Timing Is Everything

Alison R. Solomon

Wild Girl Press

This work is a work of fiction. While the town of Gulfport, Florida is a real place, any references to events, businesses, organizations and locales are intended only to give the fiction a sense of reality and authenticity. Any semblances of actual persons, living or dead, are entirely coincidental.

Copyright©2018 by Alison R. Solomon

Copyeditor: Elizabeth Andersen
Cover Design: Cindy Bamford
Back cover photo: Karen Gates

All Rights Reserved. No part of this book may be reproduced in any form by any means without the express permission of the author. This includes reprints, excerpts, photocopying, recording, or any future means of reproducing text.

Published in the United States by Wild Girl Press

ISBN: 978-0-9984400-2-6
eISBN: 978-0-9984400-3-3

DEDICATION

To everyone struggling with immigration issues everywhere

Acknowledgements

I cannot thank Michelle Lisper and Christianne Zett enough for giving so generously of their time and expertise regarding car parts and body parts. My thanks also to Officer Zach Mills, Dianna Ullery and Sylvia Martinez for their help with police procedure and immigration issues.

Some writers are very visual people. I'm not. So cover design is a painful process and I truly appreciate the patience and willingness (as well as the results!) of cover designer, Cindy Bamford, who is a pleasure to work with. Thank you also to Karen Gates for providing me with her photo of the iconic Gulfport Casino.

Thank you to copyeditor Elizabeth Andersen for her editing expertise and her kind words along the way.

My thanks to beta readers Barbara Clanton, Toni Rees, and Carol Vitelli for making me a beta, I mean better, writer.

And, as always, my deepest gratitude to my wife Carol.

PROLOGUE

February 1

Wynn

Afterward, when they asked her to describe what happened, all she could say was, "A thud and a whimper." The thud was more like an explosion, and she didn't realize until much later that she had been the one whimpering.

How many thousands of times had she taken the trash out over the course of her sixty-two years? Even though it was usually early morning when she dragged the heavy garbage can from her backyard into the alley, it wasn't unheard of for her to do it at night. There was no law against putting it out the evening before. Old Mrs. J. next door always put hers out last thing because she didn't get up until midmorning and the garbage collectors came long before that.

If only she hadn't chosen that particular moment of that particular evening to venture outside, none of this would have happened. Five minutes earlier she'd have placed the can where she always did, walked past the chopped-up tree branches Jose had piled at the side of the garage, and opened the back gate. Then she would have stepped inside the backyard and whistled at the dogs who would have come running from their favorite corner of the yard where they'd just peed against their favorite plants. After that, all three of them would have hurried through the mudroom into the house and gone to bed just like they did every night.

It didn't even have to be five minutes earlier. Just one minute and she'd have been safely inside the gate, calling Queen and Latifah to her. Instead, while her dogs were safely inside the yard alternately barking and whining, she lay on the other side of the fence, smashed against the woodpile, her arms pinned beneath her, the pain in her head so sharp it felt like her friend Sherry had taken all the knives from her blade-sharpening business and stuck them inside her brain. She had a feeling blood was oozing from various parts of her body and she was having difficulty breathing. She couldn't seem to feel her legs at all.

She tried to call out, but her chest hurt too much, and anyway she'd never make herself heard over the dogs. Besides, didn't she always tell everyone how dead her little street on the edge of Gulfport was at night? Usually she was glad for the evening peace and quiet as she sat on her porch listening to crickets and the rustle of palm fronds in the breeze, happy that she didn't live in the center of town where the loud music from Salty's and the incessant chatter of happy drinkers at O'Maddy's would have rattled her bones and kept her awake.

She heard a noise and felt a vibration and realized that she was groaning. Let the pain stop! Surely someone would rescue her soon. Wouldn't Donte hear the dogs and come outside to see what the commotion was? If only he weren't so accommodating. Just the other day Wynn had apologized for the late-night barking and Donte had told her not to worry about it, that he never paid any attention, barely even heard it. On the other side was Old Mrs. J. Wynn couldn't see whether the elderly neighbor's trash cans were lined up in the alley or not. If they were, Wynn was doomed because once the trash was out Mrs. J. would have taken out her hearing aids and been quite oblivious to everything. Wynn wondered when everyone had started referring to her neighbor as "Old Mrs. J." instead of just Mrs. J. Did you reach a certain age and become officially old? When would they start calling Wynn "Old Ms. Larimer?"

Her head was throbbing, her legs were numb, the pain in her arms was excruciating, and she desperately wanted to drift into a pain-induced sleep. She knew enough to know she mustn't, so she forced herself to keep thinking.

Why hadn't the car stopped before it hit her? The driver must have seen her. First of all, it wasn't that dark a night. She hadn't bothered with a flashlight because the light from the half-moon was strong enough to light up the alley. Even without that, the driver must surely have been able to see her since his headlights had definitely been on. There was no question in her mind about that. As she'd deposited the trash cans and turned back toward the house, the dazzle from the car's beams had completely blinded her. She'd turned her head away, assuming that the car would stop, and the next thing she knew she was being crushed into the woodpile.

Wouldn't any decent human being have stopped to offer help? Why did the driver just carry on down the alley as if nothing had happened? She felt rage rising up inside her. What kind of a person did that? The anger was partly directed at the driver and partly at herself. She could have waited until morning to put the trash out. But she'd done it tonight so that she could get up early tomorrow and go straight to work without any interruptions. She had so many jewelry orders to fulfill for Valentine's Day it was overwhelming. The kids were always nagging her to get organized, so she'd taken their advice. She'd created a list and a schedule for the following day so nothing would distract her. Not even taking out the trash.

It wasn't as if she didn't know how to make lists. When she was a teenager, her home economics teacher had taught her class how to prepare dinner. Before they started cooking, the first thing they had to do was list all the tasks involved, then break them into steps and write out a detailed schedule: when to peel the potatoes, at what point to put the pie in the oven, when to cut the bread. Everything had to be thought out so it would all come together at exactly the right time for when the assumed husband came home from work. Even back then she'd been pretty sure there would be no husband, but the planning process had been useful. Over the years, she'd forgotten all about it until recently when her daughters told her in no uncertain terms that now that they were off to college she had to find a way to get herself organized since they would no longer be home to help her. They left in September and she muddled through all the December holiday orders, getting them done only by pulling several all-nighters. That's what made her decide this next holiday, Valentine's Day, would be different.

The list for tomorrow was sitting on the drafting table in her studio. Above it, little papers with individual orders were hanging on a clothesline she'd strung up. (She'd stolen the idea from Kat's restaurant where they clipped all the food orders to a clothesline and the short-order cooks picked them off one at a time.) Her tools were laid out and everything was ready for her to cut, clip, twist and cajole metals, stones, gems, clasps and chains into the beautiful pieces her customers expected. And now as she lay crushed against the woodpile, she knew for certain none of that would happen. Three years of slogging away to create a successful business, and in a few seconds a stranger had just blown it to pieces.

She heard a car in the street and for a moment her heart lifted. If only the driver would turn up the alley. But they didn't. Why would they? No one ever drove up the alley at night. Apart from the jerk who'd used his car against her like a battering ram.

She'd been so pleased with herself for creating tomorrow's list that her reward had been to take out a bottle of pinot noir and call Michaela. Sipping wine and catching up on Mikki's exploits was the best way to end any evening. Wynn was so proud of both her daughters, and when you thought about how far they'd come and what they'd had to endure, it was pretty amazing that they were so well-adjusted. Most moms complained that their daughters were taciturn and didn't want to share anything with them, but Mikki was such an open book that sometimes it was hard to get her off the phone. They'd had such a lovely conversation this evening, but then it started getting late and Wynn felt guilty because she knew she had to get up early the next day, so she told Mikki she needed to end the call.

"But Mom, don't you want to hear about this really cool yoga class I took yesterday?" There was a wounded tone to Mikki's voice, but Wynn reassured her that not only would she hear about it next time they talked, but she'd also look forward to finding out what happened to Mikki's best friend, who'd been accused of plagiarism. Now she wished she hadn't been in such a hurry, or that Mikki would remember something she needed to tell Wynn and call back. It wouldn't help though. If she rang and Wynn didn't answer, Mikki would assume she'd placed the phone on silent and gone to bed.

The dogs were still barking and she could hear them both jumping up and down against the fence. She was always trying to get Queen to shut up, but for once she was happy her dog was so badly behaved. Or perhaps it wasn't bad behavior at all; this time Queen was looking out for her. What about the Russian couple across the street? Wouldn't they wonder what was going on? She never spoke to them beyond saying hello because they barely spoke a word of English, but surely they'd know how to call an ambulance?

How long had she been lying there? She was starting to feel cold. She'd padded out in only her pajamas and slippers, thinking it would only take a minute, but the slippers had flown off when she was hurled into the woodpile and the pajamas weren't enough to keep her warm on such a chilly evening. Only a few hours earlier she'd crowed delightedly to Mikki that the temperature was going to fall into the thirties overnight, a rare occurrence in this part of Florida.

"Finally we're having a real winter!" She'd smiled, excited that she could wear something other than the flimsy nightshirts she lived in for ten months of the year. Now she wondered how long she could lie there, cold and injured. The light from Mrs. J's bedroom went out, and Wynn felt hope drain from her. Her body started shaking, and the shock and anger she'd been feeling began to morph into something else.

Fear.

What if no one found her until it was too late?

PART ONE

PART ONE

CHAPTER ONE

One month earlier

Kat

"Come to the mingle tonight," Cindy told Kat as they left The Garrett, the hotel where Kat was a chef and Cindy a waitress. "It'll be fun, and they're raffling off tickets for the Lady in Red ball." Kat slung her jacket over her shoulder as they walked down the street, enjoying the feeling of warm air on her bare arms. It was early January but the temperature was balmy, not unusual for their little town of Gulfport, Florida.

"Why? I'd much rather stay home, make a big bowl of popcorn and watch a movie with Pnina purring happily on my lap."

"That's your problem. You've forgotten what it's like to make a woman purr instead of your cat." Cindy unzipped the overly warm jacket she'd worn this morning, hedging her bets on the weather. "For once you're not working the evening shift, so come on out with us. I heard there's live music."

Kat shrugged. She wasn't a dancer. She watched with envy as other women swayed their hips in ways that made dancing look like the most natural thing in the world. When she tried, she was pretty sure she looked like a marionette being jerked around by an unseen puppeteer.

"Maybe you'll meet someone new." Cindy said, putting her

arm through Kat's as they walked past the art gallery with the giant mermaid in the window.

"Maybe I don't want to."

Kat tried to continue walking, but Cindy pulled on her arm and twisted her around. "You can't withdraw from the world of dating forever. One negative experience doesn't mean you should never try again."

"It's been a lot more than one, and I would hardly call what happened with the last one just a bad experience."

"You've been feeling sorry for yourself for long enough. I'm not taking no for an answer tonight. The whole gang will be there and I promised Jan and Deirdre I'd get you to come. If you don't, I owe them a year's supply of gelato." Cindy had recently started experimenting with homemade ice cream and was determined to come up with flavors no one had ever tried before.

"You want to make extravagant bets with people? That's not my problem." Kat knew she sounded belligerent though she didn't mean to. Cindy was just trying to look out for her. "How come you never offered me the same deal?"

"Fine. I will. If you come tonight, I'll bring you a gallon of different-flavored ice cream once a week for a month."

"A month? That's it?"

Cindy shook her head. "Take it or leave it."

"I'll take it. What time does this shindig start? And what do I wear?"

"Wear anything you like. I'll pick you up at seven." They reached the corner where they both went in different directions. "By the way," said Cindy as she turned to the right, "I didn't really make that bet with Jan and Deirdre. Even I'm not that crazy."

***

The gang was all there by the time Kat joined them at their table at the Dolphin's Dive. Cindy smiled warmly while Jan looked her up and down.

"I'm glad you dressed up." Jan's dark eyes had an expression of amusement tinged with disapproval. Kat looked down at her "Keep Gulfport Weird" sweatshirt and olive green cargo shorts and compared them with Jan's regal appearance. Naturally Jan's hair was perfectly braided, and her flowing Indian print pants made her look even taller and more beautiful than she already was.

"It's not like I'm gonna meet the love of my life tonight," she muttered, watching Linda, the hostess for tonight's mingle, walk across the patio, her arm slung around a woman Kat had never seen before.

Linda grinned broadly as she approached the table where they were seated underneath an enormous ficus plant.

"Fresh meat!" She said extricating her arm from around the woman and nudging her toward their table. The new woman looked embarrassed. Her eyes widened and she pushed her hand awkwardly through a thick mane of dark hair. Kat found her gaze traveling the length of the stranger's body, from her wavy mahogany curls, high cheek bones, and penetrating dark eyes to the curvy hips that swelled beyond her sleek leather jacket.

"Don't worry, she's just joking," Cindy said to the woman. "Please join us."

Linda introduced the newcomer by name, but Kat couldn't catch it.

"Adriela?" Kat tried to make her voice heard above the chatter of fifty loud lesbians.

The woman shook her head. "Gabriella."

Kat jumped up and pulled back a chair for her, and Gabriella slithered awkwardly into it. Kat wracked her mind for an intelligent conversation opener but was saved by the clang of an electric guitar chord and the announcement that the live music was starting. Everyone at the table rose while Gabriella looked around her, apparently unsure if she should join them.

"Want to dance?" Kat asked, shocking herself. She was inordinately pleased when Gabriella nodded her head and stood. Pippa and the band were playing a salsa, and as soon as they hit the floor it was clear Gabriella was one of those natural dancers Kat envied so much. She'd always longed to be able to get her hips to sway the way Gabriella's were. Some women seemed to have it in their bones, their hips moving effortlessly, their hands flat against the air. At least Kat wasn't the only one who couldn't do it properly. Most of the women just did their usual 1980s boogie or whatever steps they pleased. Gabriella had closed her eyes, but by the smile playing on her lips Kat could see the pleasure she took in dancing. Kat would have liked to move closer, maybe place her hand on Gabriella's hip or shoulder, but in dancing—and she guessed in life too—Kat always let her partner take the lead.

Gabriella opened her eyes when the salsa was replaced by a

slow dance. Kat hesitated for a moment and then said, "Shall we sit?" She wasn't sure if Gabriella looked relieved or disappointed.

They both grabbed a bottle of beer from the bucket on the table.

"Tell me about you," Kat said.

Gabriella shrugged. "I've lived in Florida for many years but I started life in Mexico. America's my home now. Always will be."

Kat smiled in delight. "Me too. I mean, not that I'm from Mexico, but I also grew up somewhere else. My mom brought me here from Israel when I was eight. You don't have an accent."

"We all have accents." It could have been a rebuke, but Gabriella's eyes were warm as she said it.

"I know. I can't believe I said that to you because that's exactly what I always tell people. Just because someone doesn't have a southern twang or a Louisiana drawl or a foreign inflection doesn't mean they don't have an accent. But yours isn't at all Mexican sounding."

"You're right. Even when I lived in Mexico, I was already practicing my American accent. Nowadays I think in English first, before Spanish, and I remember when I woke up one day and thought, "wow, I even dream in English!" She took a slug of beer, throwing her head back. "You don't sound Israeli."

"No. I got my accent knocked out of me pretty quickly in elementary school." Kat closed her eyes for a moment, remembering the circle of kids who laughed because she couldn't pronounce the sound "th" when she said her favorite cookies were "tin mints."

"We'll have to call you Kat on a hot tin roof!" said the girl's mom and everyone started clawing in the air. Kat didn't understand the literary reference, but she still felt herself flush hot with shame when she remembered the incident. She pulled herself back to the present.

"Now we have two things in common." Kat said. "We grew up somewhere else, and we don't have accents that match our place of birth. I love meeting people from other countries, probably because I love to travel. My goal in life is to visit every continent in the world, even Antarctica."

"I can't believe you said that. It's my goal too." Gabriella's eyes sparkled and Kat was aware of a little flutter in the base of her stomach.

"I wasn't going to come tonight." She blurted out. "My friend Cindy bullied me into it. Now I'm glad I did." She hoped she didn't sound too forward, but she *was* glad. Maybe she was ready to move on.

"Me neither. I've never been to anything like this before. But I need to meet new people, create new friends."

"You've come to the right place. You can't get friendlier than Gulfport," said Kat, still trying to quell the waves rippling through her stomach. "What do you do for a living?" she asked.

"I work at a nursing home. But let's not talk about work. I like to volunteer when I can at a food bank downtown."

"The Gulf Coast Food Bank?"

"You've heard of it?" Gabriella looked surprised. "Most people don't know it exists unless they need it."

"I'm a chef for a restaurant and I've also done some private gigs. When there are large amounts of leftovers, I ask my customers if they'd like to donate them to the local shelter. But if the food's still packaged, we always give it to the food bank. I definitely haven't ever run into you. I'd remember if I had," Kat said, a grin spreading across her face.

"Now we have three things in common. Or four. I lost count." Gabriella beamed. She had one of those smiles that didn't stop at her mouth, but spread across her face. "I wouldn't have pegged you as a chef though. You're so small. Don't you eat your creations?"

"Sure I do. I have one of those natural metabolisms that keeps me this size."

"Then that's something we don't have in common. I've always been . . . curvy. My whole family is. When I was a child, kids used to tease me all the time and call me *gordita*, fatso. So then my parents decided it would be my nickname."

"Your parents nicknamed you fatso? That's cruel."

"No, no, it's also a term of affection. I don't know, like calling someone my little plump one, or something. It was a way to reclaim the term as something positive."

"Do they still call you that?"

"I shortened it to Gordy when I became fascinated by all things American, and that's what I've been at home ever since. You can call me Gordy if you like. All the people closest to me do." She paused. "Oh . . . I mean . . ."

Kat laughed. "Of course we're going to be close. But now, Senorita Gordy, here's the real test to see how alike we are. My specialty is pastry and dessert. If you could have any dessert in the world, what would it be?"

Gabriella sat back and took a slug of her beer. "That's easy. Though it's probably not anything you've even tasted, let alone made."

"I doubt that. Tres leches? Flan?"

She shook her head. "You're not even on the right track. You're right that it's not American. But it's not Mexican either."

"Cherpumple? Bienmesabe cake?"

Gabriella—Gordy's face took on a look of confusion. "I'm sure you're an expert at both of those, whatever they are. Nope. Something much simpler, though nobody's ever heard of it. Gooseberry fool."

Kat gasped and felt her stomach flip. Gordy was the first person she'd ever met who voiced this choice. Kat adored gooseberry fool. Americans had no idea what a fruit fool was, but Kat had discovered it when her mom took her and her brother to England one summer. When she tried to describe it to friends, she had to use words like parfait and mousse, but it still didn't translate. How could this woman know that Kat had once proudly proclaimed that anyone who married her would have to be a fan of gooseberries since they were her favorite fruit?

"It's my favorite dessert too." Kat's voice came out in a whisper.

Gordy looked taken aback. "Well, you did say you enjoy traveling, so I shouldn't be surprised. I suppose next you'll tell me that your all-time favorite movie is *Gone with the Wind*. Mine is, even though it's so completely politically incorrect. There are so many reasons to disapprove of the movie—and trust me I do—but I just can't get enough of Miss Scarlett O'Hara."

The hairs on the back of Kat's neck separated and she could almost feel them rise one by one. She nodded and lowered her voice to a whisper. "Me too. Though I've never admitted that to someone I just met." She grinned. "But I can't help it. I love that movie."

Kat felt as if she couldn't catch her breath. There was no denying that the woman sitting opposite her was beautiful. She'd removed her leather jacket when they danced and a close-fitting black tank top had revealed an ample bosom, a body that tapered at the waist and then flared into wide hips. When Gordy swept her lush hair behind her ear, the gesture appeared unselfconscious as if she weren't aware that it revealed a long neck and buff shoulders. But it wasn't just her looks. Kat couldn't remember ever meeting someone with whom she'd felt so instantly connected. Gordy was looking directly at her, and those soft brown eyes seemed to pierce her soul. Maybe that was how she knew exactly what Kat liked: she could see all the way inside her.

Kat decided to try one more thing. "Hiking?" she asked, trying to inflect an air of nonchalance into her voice.

Gordy nodded. "Love it! Diana Krall's *Love Scenes*?" This time it was Kat who shook her head with wonder, but nodded affirmatively at the same time. "Absolutely."

They stared, then both started talking at the same time, stopped and started again.

"Soccer or football?" Kat asked.

"No question. Soccer." Kat nodded. Maybe it was because neither of them had grown up in the US. "And I'm totally into tennis," said Gordy.

Kat thought momentarily of her friend Wynn whose daughters had both won tennis scholarships to college. Kat was glad to hear that Gordy liked tennis because she wanted Wynn to like anyone she would date. And right now, she had no doubt that's where she and Gordy were headed. "Venus or Serena?"

"Close call. Serena's so strong, but I love the grace and beauty of Venus."

Kat nodded, and for a moment they both stared at each other. Kat could feel her cheeks getting hot, along with other parts of her body too. It wasn't just that they had everything in common; it was that Gordy was beautiful and sexy and, unless she was completely misreading the situation, flirting as much as Kat was.

Cindy returned to her seat and spoke to Gordy. "How come you stopped dancing? You looked great out there." She glanced at Kat, raised her eyebrows, and turned back to Gordy. "Or did my friend force you to keep her company here instead?"

Gordy laughed, and for a while everyone at the table chatted about the latest celebrity news. When the others got up to dance again, Kat hung back. She wanted Gordy all to herself. Besides, she knew what a dork she looked like when she was on the dance floor.

The first time around Gordy had been busy looking around, but Kat didn't want to give her a second opportunity to see how uncoordinated she really was.

When it was just the two of them, Kat turned back to Gordy. "Now for the important stuff. I want kids. At least three."

Gordy's reaction wasn't what she expected. She grabbed her phone and leaped up, a look of horror spasming across her face.

"I have to leave!" She grabbed her purse, slung it over her shoulder and started for the door.

"But—"

"Sorry," Gordy said, and bolted.

§

Kat lay in bed, trying to calm down enough to go to sleep. But every time she closed her eyes all she could see was Gordy's look of horror when Kat mentioned wanting three kids. It was so stupid of her. Why had she done it? Whoever talked about kids on a first meeting? She sat up and pulled her patchwork quilt up to her chest. She didn't really need it tonight, but Gulfport weather being the tropical paradise it was, she'd only have a couple of months before she'd be back to sweating under a thin cotton sheet.

Kat replayed the evening in her head. She started at the moment when Gordy had shrugged off her leather jacket to reveal forearms with exactly the right amount of muscle tone to show she was fit, but not steroid-fit. She moved on to the part where Gordy's hips swayed in a way that was both completely natural and incredibly sexy. She paused at the conversation where everything pointed to the fact that she and Gordy were a perfect match.

She'd let herself get carried away. Why on earth had she told someone she barely knew that she wanted three kids? Gordy wasn't stupid—she knew Kat had been flirting with her. To blurt out about kids was like proposing marriage, or worse maybe. It sounded ridiculous, and of course it had scared Gordy away. Although she could have been a little less dramatic about it. Voiced an opinion about not wanting kids, or jokingly suggest that they start with one. She didn't have to bolt like that.

Now she was gone, and Kat didn't even have a phone number. If she'd had time to ask for one, she'd be calling her right now, explaining that it was stupid, it didn't mean anything. That she wanted to get to know Gordy better and hoped she'd get a second chance. The irony was that it was the first time she'd felt attracted to anyone for ages. Just the thought of Gordy smiling at her brought a barrage of butterflies to her stomach.

Calm down. She sighed. *The last time those butterflies swarmed, it didn't turn out too well.*

CHAPTER TWO

Gabriella

Gordy charged up the path of the home she had shared until recently with her ex and rang the doorbell. The door opened immediately. Obviously, Dana had been standing right by it, waiting for her.

"I'll sue for full custody if you do this again." Her ex looked furious, and Gordy knew Dana would have been standing with both hands firmly planted on her hips if she weren't holding their slumbering six-year-old son in her arms.

"I'm sorry. I didn't mean to be so late. Time got away from me."

"What was it this time? Some former colleague with a client sob story? A billing issue that couldn't wait until morning?"

Gordy shook her head. She hated to say where she'd been but they'd agreed to always be completely honest with each other. Not being honest had led to the rupture of their relationship, and they both knew they had to put that behind them for Sammy's sake.

"I—I decided, since I live in Gulfport now, to try one of those gatherings for women."

"You were late because you spent the evening with a bunch of hairy-legged old-time lesbian hippies?" Dana snorted. "I wouldn't have thought you'd last more than ten minutes with them."

"It was fun. I—"

Timing Is Everything

"I don't have time for this." Dana handed the sleeping boy over to Gordy and picked up his backpack, thrusting it toward Gordy who looked at her helplessly. Dana shoved it over Gordy's left shoulder and slammed the front door. They headed down the garden path, Dana to her sports coupe and Gordy to her Hyundai.

"Were you kidding when you said you'd sue?" asked Gordy. "I thought we had an agreement."

"No, I wasn't." Dana turned toward Gordy, a fierce expression in her eyes. "Yes, we have an agreement. The nights I have Sammy, you can strut your stuff or pull whatever shit you want, but if I'm working the late shift and you want me to babysit for the evening, you damn well better be on time. I'm not getting reprimanded again for being late. Especially not now when I'm up for a promotion. I mean it. Do this to me again and I'll call my lawyer." She jumped into her Mirada and gunned the engine, leaving Gordy to struggle with the door to her SUV so she could place Sammy gently inside.

Gordy turned the key and sighed. She hoped desperately that Dana hadn't forgotten the promise she'd made when they agreed to separate—that they'd settle everything between them with no outside interference. Dana knew there was no going through the legal system, at least not yet. Hopefully, it wouldn't be for much longer.

After she put Sammy to bed, Gordy thought about the evening and how surprising it had been. She smiled as she relived walking into the Dolphin Dive and being instantly overwhelmed by the sight of so many women in one place. Old, young, black, brown, white—she thought she was at one of those women's festivals she'd heard about but never attended. She'd searched for a familiar face but wasn't surprised that there weren't any. These women didn't look anything like the young, fashionable crowd who drank shots and danced the salsa at La Morena in Tampa where she and Dana used to go before they had Sammy and things started going south. The women here were dressed in T-shirts and jeans, uninterested in making a fashion statement of any kind, and they mostly nursed cokes or beers. La Morena was a dark nightclub with booths set back from a small dance floor, lit only by strobe lights and pulsating with music. The Dolphin Dive was an indoor/outdoor restaurant-bar where groups of women stood or sat together in friendly groups. Dana had stood around awkwardly until one of the mingle organizers came up and rescued her.

"Can I give you a name tag?" the woman had asked, marker and labels in hand. Gordy didn't want to take the label, but everyone was wearing them and she had to admit that it made it easier to know who was part of the mingle. She allowed the woman to slap the tag on her chest and then walk her over to a group of women who were sitting at one of the tables. As they crossed the room, she felt embarrassingly overdressed. Because it was cool, she'd worn her leather jacket and a pair of ankle boots. She'd swept her wavy, black tresses behind her ears so her dangling silver cross earrings would be visible, and she'd applied the new makeup she'd treated herself to when it was on sale at Nordstrom the previous week, turning her lips into a scarlet slash. As the woman walked her to a table, she noticed that while some of the women looked presentable enough, no one else was wearing leather and most of them looked like they wouldn't know what to do with a tube of mascara if Heidi Klum herself presented them with it.

When the motley group started dancing, Gordy couldn't help imagining the disparaging comments Dana would make. At the clubs she and her ex used to frequent, no one would have gotten up to dance unless they could do a perfect salsa or merengue. Here some were doing moves that surely hadn't been seen since the era of Motown and rock and roll, while others were two-stepping and cavorting in any direction they pleased.

The surprises had kept coming. Who'd have thought a scruffy-looking redhead in a well-worn sweatshirt would set her pulse racing? Flirting with Kat had been almost like a new experience. It was almost ten years since she'd been single, and Gordy could barely remember how to do it. She had mostly relied on batting her long eyelashes and smiling.

It had been amazing to find they had so much in common. Their backgrounds, their likes and dislikes, their love of children. She couldn't wait to see Kat again. Was it too late to call her? She reached for her phone and then realized. ¡Dios mío! She'd jumped up in such a hurry she never got a phone number, nor even a last name. In fact, she'd never even told Kat why she was leaving. She'd been so absorbed in the evening that it was only when Kat mentioned children that she remembered Dana was working late shift and she needed to pick Sammy up.

She would have to find Kat and tell her the truth. But what could she say—oops I forgot my kid? It made her sound like a terrible parent. She could blame it on the fact that Dana didn't have regular shifts, that her schedule changed every week, and that they had a fluid child-care schedule, but it would only be half the truth. The other half was that she'd been so taken by Kat, she'd simply forgotten everything else.

CHAPTER THREE

Kat

"You looked awfully cozy with that new gal last night. What was her name again?"

Cindy and Kat were in the hotel kitchen getting ready for the lunch crowd. Kat was preparing vegetable soup and Cindy was pulling flatware from the deep wooden drawers of the old cabinets.

Kat felt herself blush as she answered. "Gabriella." She kept her head down and pulled onions from a string bag so she could peel them.

Cindy's eyes narrowed. "Ga-bri-el-la," she smacked her tongue against the roof of her mouth making a lapping sound with each consonant. "Gorgeous Gabriella . . ." She licked her lips. "Luscious—"

"Stop!" Kat shook an onion in Cindy's face.

Cindy looked at her closely. "Do I hear wedding bells?"

"Maybe."

Cindy's eyes widened. "I was joking."

"I know. But I wasn't. She's the One with a capital O. Not only is she fascinating, she may also be the most beautiful woman I've ever met." As soon as the words left her lips, Kat put down her knife and clapped her hand over her mouth. She and Cindy were such good friends she sometimes forgot that they'd dated for almost a year.

Cindy folded her arms across her chest as if she were

offended. Kat hoped it was in jest.

"You know you're gorgeous," Kat injected quickly, "in a different way." Cindy was barely five foot, while Gordy had a presence that made her look even taller than she was. Being with Cindy had been the only time Kat, at five foot four, had ever been the tall one in a relationship and it had always felt odd. Gordy had thick, long, dark tresses while Cindy's black hair was short and silky. Gordy's eyes were a soft brown and framed by long, curvy eyelashes, while Cindy's dark eyes were deep-set with barely any eyelashes at all. The only thing they had in common was that they weren't Caucasian. Cindy's family was originally from Vietnam.

Kat always found herself drawn to women who might be perceived as outsiders in some way. She'd been in the US for decades and everyone assumed she enjoyed all the privileges of being white, but as she often pointed out to other people, "I could never be president." The irony was that when she did travel to her homeland, she felt totally out of place there too. While green-eyed, red-headed Israelis weren't unheard of, dark-haired, dark-skinned Gordy would look much more like a native "sabra" than Kat.

"I need you to help me find her," Kat said. She took a fresh onion in her hand and placed it carefully on the board. "I couldn't sleep all night, just thinking about her."

Cindy picked up a napkin to wrap around the flatware. "If she was so amazing, why didn't you get her number?"

"I was going to. I started to tell her how many kids I want, and before I could continue she just jumped up and ran off."

Cindy took the napkin in her hand and flipped it at Kat, cuffing her ear. "How many kids . . . ? Are you nuts? Did you also ask if you could bring the U-Haul and move in while you were at it?"

"It wasn't like that. Up until that point it was incredible. We had a special bond, I could tell."

"So special that one mention of kids and she ran away?"

Kat brought her knife down on a potato with a thwack, and the half she wasn't holding skidded off the table. She bent over and picked it up. "I think she must have misunderstood. That's why I want to find her. To explain myself."

"What's to misunderstand? You meet someone, tell her you want three kids, and now you want to stalk her. I think she understood perfectly."

"No. I need your help."

"What's the rush? Let it simmer and hopefully she'll come back to the mingle next month."

"I can't wait that long! It's Valentine's Day soon. If we're going to be together, I want to do something special for it."

"No pressure on the poor woman then." Cindy grinned as she pulled a new pile of laundered napkins toward her. "Can I say something?"

Kat looked askance. "Nothing's ever stopped you before."

"For the last year you've been regaling me with tales about how your new café is going to be the best in town, but you haven't taken any of the necessary steps to start your new business. You haven't even told Frances you're thinking about quitting, which you really should since you'll be leaving eventually."

"What's that got to do with Gor-Gabriella?"

"It seems as if you're more comfortable with fantasy than with reality. You want to open a business, but you don't take the necessary steps to make it happen. You haven't been willing to even look at a woman, but now you meet a total stranger and decide she's your ticket to a perfect future, even though she didn't even give you her phone number. Why don't you come down to planet Earth and take control of the things you can?"

Kat sighed. "You don't understand. She wasn't just anyone."

Cindy finished wrapping the last of the napkins. She put them on a large silver tray and stood up. "You won't be doing yourself any favors if you waste time trying to find someone who ran away from you."

Kat waited. When Cindy still said nothing, Kat moved so that she was standing right in front of her. She cocked her head to one side and put on her best hangdog expression.

"Please?"

Cindy grimaced. "What do you need me to do?"

"You're the queen of social media. Someone has to know who she is. How many local Gabriellas can there be?"

"I'll start looking, but only on condition you tell Frances that at some point in the not too distant future you'll be handing in your notice."

"I'm not ready."

Cindy picked up the tray. "Your choice," she said as she headed to the door.

Timing Is Everything

Kat felt her stomach lurch at the thought of telling Frances. The hotel owner had been so good to her. What if she didn't find a suitable location for months? Suppose Frances found a replacement before Kat was ready to go? But she had to find Gordy, and Cindy was the one to help her. Nobody was on social media more than her.

"Fine," she said. "You work your magic and I'll tell Frances."

§

"You're sure you posted it everywhere you could?" The shift was almost over and Kat couldn't wait any longer. She'd been asking Cindy every hour. Even though their boss disapproved, Cindy had a way of being able to stay on top of her social media even in the middle of the busiest shift.

"I told you already. A friend of a Facebook friend said she knew a woman named Gabriella, but when I checked out her profile she was nothing like the chick who came to the Dolphin Dive."

"And you tried all those other things you do—neighborhood groups, Twitter, whatever they are?"

Cindy drummed her fingers on the serving table, waiting for the order Kat was preparing.

"Be patient! Something will come up. If you really hit it off, she'll come looking for you, won't she?" Cindy asked as she picked up an order of fried green tomatoes and jalapeño cornbread. Kat tossed the crepe she was frying, then sprinkled cheese and mushrooms onto it.

"How? We only go to the Dolphin once a month. I don't want to wait that long. And if she's looking for me on social media, you know I don't use my real name."

"Maybe it's about time you did."

Kat sighed. She'd been such an open, trusting person. Until last year when she'd been forced to recognize that people weren't always who you thought they were.

"Meanwhile, did you tell Frances?" Cindy looked at her friend directly.

Kat lowered her head "I'm going to." She plated the crepe and pushed it toward Cindy. "I promise."

Cindy picked up the plate at the same time the door swung

open and Frances entered. "Here's your chance." Cindy whispered loudly as she pushed her butt against the swing door and swiveled to walk through it into the restaurant.

"Your chance to do what?" Frances asked, a smile playing on her lips.

Kat shook her head. "Ignore her. What's up?"

"I just had a phone call. I gather you're on the wanted list." Shit. Was it someone with information about a possibility for her new restaurant? She never gave out her work number, but everyone knew where she worked. She'd better tell Frances before she lost her chance.

"I—I've been meaning to . . . it's just that . . ." She knotted her eyebrows, thinking what she could say and how to say it. She needed to get the words right.

Frances came over and put her hand on Kat's arm. "Don't look so panic-stricken. I was joking."

"Oh."

"You had a call is all. Some gal named Gabriella. Said she'd spent the day calling every restaurant in town trying to track you down."

"Gabriella called?" It was as if the sun had suddenly burst through a cloud and the heat of it was warming every part of her. "Did you give her my phone number?"

"I told her I couldn't confirm or deny if you were an employee, because that's confidential information—"

"No!" Now it was Kat's turn to grab Frances's arm.

"I wasn't about to tell her anything. Especially after what happened last year." Kat's heart sank. Was that going to haunt her forever? "But don't panic. I got her phone number for you and told her that if such a person worked here and if such a person wanted to contact her . . ."

Frances couldn't get the next words out because Kat was already flinging her arms around her. Frances laughed and extricated herself, pulling out a scrap of paper from her pocket and thrusting it toward Kat who grabbed it quickly.

As Frances turned to go back to the office, she paused, her hand on the door. "What was it you've been meaning to tell me?" She asked, a puzzled expression on her face.

"Oh." Kat paused. "Nothing," she said quickly. "Like you, I was joking. Thanks for the phone number. You're my shero."

CHAPTER FOUR

January 31

Wynn

Wynn nodded to the familiar faces at BusNet, her business networking meeting, as she walked in and took her seat at one of the tables that had been set up in a U shape so everyone could see and hear each other. Unsurprisingly, Kat wasn't there yet. Wynn had noticed that Kat, who was generally an extremely reliable person, always seemed to run a little late for these meetings. Wynn suspected she knew why. Kat talked about wanting to open her cafe, but she wasn't doing what it took to make it happen, and these networking meetings were all about holding each other accountable.

Wynn smiled to herself as she remembered the first time Kat came to BusNet. She'd sauntered through the door in her khaki cargo shorts and a T-shirt that encouraged those viewing it to "Keep Gulfport Weird." She'd paused in the doorway and raised her eyebrows. Whatever she'd expected, apparently it wasn't men and women in business suits and power dresses. She looked for a moment as if she were going to bolt right back through the doorway she'd entered, but then a look of determination had swept her face and she'd marched herself to a chair and sat down.

They all had thirty seconds to introduce themselves and Wynn had been impressed with Kat's "elevator speech."

"I'm currently a chef at a renowned hotel restaurant in Gulfport, but within six months I'm going to be the owner and operator of Kit-Kat's Tea Emporium." She'd sounded self-confident and assured, and had even outlined a brief version of her business plan to them. Wynn had been impressed with the younger woman, as well as excited to hear that Gulfport was getting a new hangout. At the end of the meeting, she'd approached Kat and introduced herself. They'd gone out for coffee and quickly discovered that in addition to having plenty in common, they clicked on a personal level. Despite the twenty-five year age difference, Wynn now considered Kat one of her close friends.

Dave called the meeting to order just as Kat slipped in and took her seat next to Wynn.

"A reminder to everyone that after introductions Madge is doing the main presentation and Wynn and Bernie are today's brain-pickers."

Damn. She'd completely forgotten. Every week two people got to talk about whatever problems they were having and ask for advice and suggestions for how to resolve them. While everyone went around the room doing funny, witty or boring introductions, Wynn quickly scribbled some notes to herself. What was her biggest problem right now? Money. Ever since the girls had started college, money was tight. Having two daughters in their first year of college turned out to be a lot more expensive than she'd expected. She had wanted them each to go to the college of their choice, even though it would have been a lot more cost effective for Wynn if they'd gone to the same one. Instead, there were two gas tanks that needed to be filled and two dorm rooms that needed all kinds of extras. She'd naively thought that since both girls had scholarships and financial aid everything would be covered, but it turned out there were numerous things like transportation, gas, and school supplies that weren't part of the deal.

The introductions were finished. "Before Madge has the floor, who'd like to go first? Bernie or Wynn?" Pam, the person leading the meeting today, swiveled on her five-inch heels as she turned to Bernie and Wynn. Pam was an SEO expert. Wynn hadn't even known what Search Engine Optimization was when she first came to these meetings, but she'd quickly discovered that SEO experts were in extremely high demand, especially if they could prove they were driving potential buyers to their clients' websites.

Wynn intimated that Bernie should go first. She needed more time to figure out how best to use the expertise of the group. If she told them she needed more money, they'd tell her to raise her prices. She probably could do that and still have plenty of customers, but charging a fair price for her custom-made jewelry had always been an ethical issue for her. Maybe it wasn't about the money so much as it was about time. Wynn had more than enough jewelry orders to cover her expenses if she could just make time to get them all done. Valentine's Day was still a few weeks away and she was already inundated with orders. Could the group help her figure out how to get more time in her schedule?

When it was her turn to ask for advice, Wynn stood up.

"As most of you know, I own a home with a large yard, and I have two dogs. My daughters used to help out with the vegetable garden, the weeding, and the dogs, but now that they're away, it's just me. I also have to shop, cook, clean, and try to stay on top of house maintenance. I know my business should take priority, especially at this time of year when I have so many orders to fulfill, but I'm having a hard time juggling everything. Do any of you have suggestions for how to make it all work without starving myself or my dogs or succumbing to a yard that looks more like an overgrown jungle?"

People tittered, then right away started throwing out ideas. The rule was that you couldn't respond to anything they said. It was too easy to "yes but" the suggestions so Wynn bit her lip as the ideas started to flow.

"Hire a dog-walker!" Yes, she thought, but I don't have time to advertise, interview, hire someone, and explain the dogs' routines and quirks.

"Eat packaged meals for a month!" Yes, her brain said, but the only ones that were healthy enough were too expensive. Wynn could hear her yes-buts loud and clear. The group was right about not letting you speak up.

"Find a wife to take care of everything." That was Victor who owned a construction company and doubtless did have a wife who cooked and cleaned for him. Wynn could feel Kat next to her, grinning. While many in the group had probably figured out Kat was gay, most of them looked at Wynn, with her flowing, gray curls, her arms covered in bangles, and her gypsy-print skirts, and just assumed she was straight.

"Make up a schedule," Bernie said. "Write into the calendar when you're going to do things, and then stick to it."

Later that evening, Wynn called Kat. They were in the habit of calling each other the day of the BusNet meetings as a way to consolidate the ideas they'd heard discussed that day. Wynn asked Kat what she made of Bernie's idea of creating a schedule.

"I think he's right. When you're self-employed and work from home, it's too easy to get distracted. If you put everything on your schedule, it would be easier for you to see where your time goes and which things you might have to let go of. I know you have to walk Queen and Latifah, but as Ronnie said, there are other things you could forgo."

"Like what?"

Wynn was sitting in her tan leather recliner, legs tucked underneath her, absently stroking Latifah's silky head in between sipping on a glass of Chardonnay. Queen was sprawled at her feet. She was in a cozy nook that was part of her enormous bedroom, a room so enchanting it had been one of the reasons she bought the house. Unfortunately, that was before she realized how much work a yard with two mango trees, a papaya, and several bamboo trees would be. Talking on the phone was one of Wynn's favorite activities. Would she have to write that into her schedule too?

"Maybe you could buy some packaged meals once in a while."

"But I like cooking. It's relaxing."

"I know. But if you were to write on your schedule '3-4 p.m. shop, 4-6 p.m. cook,' you might see that maybe you don't have three hours to spare and that if you heated up a frozen pizza you'd have three hours to do your jewelry."

Wynn nodded. Kat was right. She probably did waste too much time doing things that gave her pleasure instead of focusing on her work. At least she could give this idea a chance for the next two weeks. "You were very quiet in the progress report part of the meeting," she said. "Have you done any of the things that were on your list?"

"I really have been checking the listings to see if there's anything coming up that I could lease."

"And is there anything?"

There was a pause. "Possibly. I'm not sure. I have to make a call."

"Then do it! Have you told Frances yet?"

There was silence on the other end, which Wynn took to mean she hadn't. She waited.

"What am I going to tell her? I might be leaving, but I don't know when? I might be starting a business that could be in competition with hers? I don't see how telling her up-front will help any. What if she gets mad and tells me to leave right away?"

"She won't. She's not vindictive, and anyway she couldn't let you go without having a replacement. Kit-Kat's isn't going to be in competition with The Garrett. It's going to be yet another delightful addition to our quirky culinary scene, but it's not going to compete with an established hotel restaurant, which specializes in southern cooking and fine dining." Wynn took a sip of wine. This wasn't the first time they'd had this conversation. She knew it was all emotional. Whatever excuse she might give, it was Kat's fear that stopped her from moving forward, not her logic. Time to change the subject.

"How's Gabriella?"

"Oh my god, Wynn, she's fantastic. In fact, I . . . well, never mind. Let's just say, I'm happier than I've been in a very long time."

"That's terrific. I'm glad for you. Just don't rush into anything."

"Why do you say that? I thought you liked her."

"I do. But you've barely known her a month. You said you were going to take it slow, so . . ."

Wynn stopped herself. She was hardly one to preach. She hadn't been in any relationship now for years. Who knew how she'd act if she thought she were in love? As if Kat could read her mind, her friend said, "You should come to a mingle some time. There are plenty of women your age. They'd be all over you."

"If I don't have time to shop and cook, I definitely don't have time for a girlfriend. You can have the romance for both of us," Wynn said. Between taking care of her daughters and her business, love had been the last thing on her mind. But what she said to Kat wasn't entirely true. She knew love wasn't something you had to make time for. It just came along and you fitted it in. But Kat wasn't the only one whose emotions held her back. Ever since Barker, Wynn hadn't attempted to have a relationship. Underneath it all was a lurking fear that made opening herself up to anyone too scary. She took another sip of wine.

"Don't worry about me, Kat. I'm happy. Maybe one of these days . . . but for now, I'm going to take everyone's advice and focus on making money."

After she hung up, Wynn took out a large pad of paper. She would do what they'd all suggested and write up a schedule. Her daughters would call her old-fashioned for not using her phone or laptop to do it, but she liked the feel of the pen in her hand and knew she'd feel more confident seeing things on paper.

The phone rang. "Mom?"

It was Mikki. Wynn put the paper and pen down. The schedule would have to wait.

CHAPTER FIVE

Gabriella

Gordy's hands were shaking as she tore open the envelope marked Department of Homeland Security. It had come to her legal address, the one she shared with Dana, who must have dropped it into her mailbox before heading to work. Just three months earlier, she and Dana had sent in all the forms, fees, and documentation needed to convert her resident status from conditional to permanent. The next stage was being contacted for a biometrics appointment where they'd fingerprint her and do a final security check. The numerous immigration manuals she'd pored over stated that it could take anywhere from six to eighteen months for that to happen. Why would they be contacting her so soon?

"I don't understand why we have to give them this material all over again," Dana had said when Gordy had given her the forms and packet of materials to sign last October. "They have all this from the first time we applied for your green card. The marriage certificate and wedding pictures haven't changed since then!"

"It's just the way the system works. We still have to prove our marriage was bona fide. It's always better to give too much documentation than not enough."

"And tell me again why you have to get a new green card instead of just applying for citizenship?"

"The card they gave me when we got married was for two

years. No one can apply for citizenship until they've had their green card for five years. So I have to convert the two-year conditional green card to a ten-year permanent one; otherwise, I'm out of status and can be deported. Once I have the ten-year one, I can apply for citizenship in three years."

"And once you get this one, we can get divorced."

"Don't say it like that. You make it sound like one of those false marriages where the only reason for the marriage was the green card."

"I'm sorry," Dana said. "We both know that it was real and I screwed up. I'd never let them think you did it just for immigration. I only meant . . . I guess a part of me still hoped you'd say we wouldn't get divorced. That you'd changed your mind. I know it's just a fantasy."

Gordy had looked at her and sighed. Her marriage had been over the day she came home and found Dana and a buff-looking woman in the living room hastily pulling on their clothes. Dana had begged and pleaded and assured her it wouldn't happen again, but Gordy had finally admitted to herself that the marriage was a mistake. The infidelity only clarified what she'd already known in her heart—that she and Dana had been in love, but they weren't anymore. The problem was that she had to stay married in order to remain in the country legally. Luckily, Dana was so contrite she agreed to support Gordy any way she could, even if it meant living separately while staying married. Dana assured Gordy that she wouldn't do anything to jeopardize Gordy's immigration status. In return, Gordy had agreed to give Dana her freedom as soon as she got her ten-year card and no longer had to stay married to be legal. She wished there were another way of doing it, but while everyone else could get married and then realize they'd made a mistake, immigrants were considered liars if they fell out of love in less than two years.

Gordy looked at the envelope in her hand. Were they denying the request for a permanent green card? Had she and Dana made a mistake on the form? Dana had wanted to use an attorney to file the forms, but Gordy had insisted it was straightforward since they'd already done it once before. Attorneys were expensive and, even without one, filing the form had cost them almost $700.

Gordy's heart was hammering. It always did whenever she got

correspondence from the Department of Homeland Security. She tore open the envelope and read the one-page notice.

A broad smile appeared on her lips. A moment later she was on the phone to Kat.

"Put on your best T-shirt and cleanest shorts. We're celebrating tonight!"

§

"I couldn't believe it! Nobody ever gets their biometrics appointment that quickly."

Despite the chill in the air, they were sitting on the patio of their favorite Italian restaurant on Beach Boulevard where purple clematis chased bright yellow jessamine up brick walls and the ocher stucco reminded Gordy of the medieval streets in Tuscany.

"What the heck is barometrics?"

"Bio, not baro. It's a fancy term for a fingerprinting appointment."

"I never met anyone who celebrated getting fingerprinted. Isn't that usually when friends start collecting bail money?"

Gordy laughed. "It means they accepted the form and documentation. Once I get fingerprinted, they'll send me the ten-year green card. And once I have that Dana and I can live apart from each other and I can file for divorce."

"I thought you already lived apart."

"We do, but not officially. The place I'm living belongs to a friend who's on sabbatical in France. Officially I still live in Kenwood."

"Wasn't it risky to move out?"

"I couldn't stay. Not after . . . It was all very serendipitous. After I realized I needed to leave, I was crying into my tequila with Mo, a former colleague who was off to France for a year, and he said I could stay at his place. There's no rental agreement, and all the bills come in his name. That's how I ended up in Gulfport."

"A toast to Mo." Kat picked up her Chianti glass and clinked it against Gordy's. "And your fingerprint date is for Valentine's Day so while everyone else is celebrating the festival of love, you'll be declaring your love for the United States by rolling your fingers and thumbs for the Citizenship and Immigration Services in Tampa."

Gordy nodded, her mouth full of crusty ciabatta, her heart as warm as the Italian bread. Everything was coming together in her life, and it had started last month when she danced a salsa with a girl who could barely jerk her limbs in rhythm. It was hard to believe how wonderful the past month had been. She'd been terrified Kat wouldn't want to speak to her again after she ran out of the Dolphin Dive. She'd been determined to find her and apologize as soon as possible. It was already one of the stories they now joked about, imagining themselves regaling their future kids with it.

"And while I couldn't figure out how to find Mami, she came looking for me!" They imagined Kat saying.

They'd agreed to take their relationship slowly, then in typical lesbian fashion had spent every spare minute they could with each other. Which wasn't as much as either would have liked because Gordy had Sammy, and Kat often worked evening shifts.

"Don't you think it's time I met your son?" Kat asked as she wound spaghetti around her fork and then plunged it into her mouth quickly before it could unravel.

Gordy paused, her fork midair. "It's not that I don't want you to. He'll love you, I'm sure of it."

"Well then . . ."

"I haven't been with anyone since Dana. I don't want to confuse him with a string of girlfriends."

Kat banged her fork down in mock anger. "A string? Do you have a posse of girls waiting in line? Is that where you are nights I don't see you?"

"No, of course not. I didn't mean I had anyone else. I meant . . . if you change your mind. I don't want to introduce him to someone and then that person leaves."

Kat's face softened. "I'm not going anywhere." She leaned across the table and took Gordy's hand. "I mean it."

"Or if something goes wrong with my green card and I can't stay . . ."

"Don't even say that! Nothing's going to go wrong. It's all smooth sailing from here. Admit that you've run out of excuses." Kat smiled, and Gordy mirrored her grin with one of her own.

"Okay. We'll make a plan with Sammy, I promise."

The waitress took their plates and asked if they wanted dessert.

Timing Is Everything

Gordy glanced at her watch. She had time for a quick coffee before she had to pick Sammy up. She ordered a decaf. Kat ordered mint tea and a cannoli, then said she'd be right back.

Gordy watched the people walking by. The temperature was pleasant, but when a couple walked by in tank tops she knew they must be snowbirds from Minnesota or Canada. Locals made the most of wearing long sleeves any time the temperature dipped below seventy. She looked at her watch again. That decaf better come soon. And Kat, too, if she didn't want to eat her cannoli alone.

Kat finally returned just as the waitress approached with their drinks and dessert. The coffee was so hot it almost scalded her.

"You took a long time," she said.

Kat smiled. "Had to take care of something."

After Gordy's coffee had cooled enough for her to drink it, she gathered up her purse. She needed to leave if she wasn't going to be late.

There was a rustling behind her and suddenly a male tenor voice rang out. She turned around.

"*O Sole Mio.*" The rich tenor belonged to a man in a red and white striped sailor's shirt and a straw boater. Kat moved her chair from opposite Gordy until she was sitting next to her, her arm around Gordy's shoulder. Gordy relaxed into Kat's body. She felt a warm glow spread through her as the singer serenaded them and Kat stroked her hair. After he'd sung in Italian, he did a verse in English and then in Spanish. Gordy listened to the translation. "*Mi sol está frente a ti.*" Gordy realized that although she understood Italian, she'd never paid attention to the lyrics before. *My own sun is on your face.* Gordy had always loved the warmth and beauty of the sun. Now she realized it was true—Kat's face was her own personal sun. But it was all happening so quickly.

"Did you like it?" Kat asked when he finished, brushing her lips against Gordy's.

"I loved it."

"But you're frowning."

"No, I'm just . . .bewildered. I don't even know how you managed to organize it so quickly and get him to sing in Spanish. More than that, I'm shocked at what's happening between us."

"Wait until Valentine's Day." Kat said. "I'm a romantic. You'll get fingerprinted and then I'm going to give you an evening to remember. But before that I can't wait to meet Sammy."

"Oh!" Gordy jumped up. "Sammy! I have to pick him up." She'd done it again. Let Kat make her lose track of time.

§

Where the fuck are you? Gordy saw the text as she sped up Beach Boulevard, racing toward Kenwood. Stopping to reply would slow her down and she was determined to get to Dana's on time, so she ignored it. A line of cars was waiting to pull into the main drag, which was surprising, but Gordy knew the area well enough to know she could avoid them by going down a side street. She pulled the steering wheel sharply to swing a right down a narrow one-way street. She was halfway down when she realized there was a U-Haul farther down completely obstructing the street. Who the heck moved at this time of night? And if they did what gave them the right to block the street? She watched as two people of undetermined gender struggled to pull a large mattress from the back of the truck. Shit. This could take awhile, especially if they had a whole lot more furniture to unload. Now what? She supposed she could try to back all the way up this street but it was narrow and she wasn't great at backing up the SUV at the best of times.

She heard a ping and looked down: *I'm gonna put Sammy out on the curb if you're not here in seven minutes.* She'd promised Dana she'd be back before ten and even though she didn't think her ex would really leave their child in the street, the second text worried her. She remembered what Dana had said the last time she was late to pick up Sammy. It was the night she met Kat. "I'll sue for full custody if you do it again."

Ahead of her to her left she saw a dirt alley that ran between the homes. She could use it to cut over to the next street. She generally avoided these alleys at night because they were dark and could be rutted, but she had no choice. She swerved left off the street feeling the gravel of the alley crunch beneath her tires. She should have explained to Kat that she didn't have time to listen to the man serenading them, however romantic it was. She didn't think Dana would put Sammy out on the street and she wasn't totally convinced her ex would really ask for full custody, but she couldn't risk either. She decided to text, just in case. She looked down at her phone. *There in ten—*, her thumbs flew across the keys and just as she was about to type *mins* she felt a massive jolt and heard a loud bang. Moments later she heard dogs barking in the distance.

She looked up in horror as the car shot forward. Shit! What the heck had she hit? She glanced in the rearview mirror and from the light reflectors made out something that looked like a large pile, though she couldn't tell of what. Had she hit it? Was that what caused the loud thud? If she hadn't been looking at her lap, texting, she'd know for sure. Meanwhile her car was still moving forward and was already at the end of the alley.

She was shaking badly. She should run back and take a quick look. What if she'd damaged something on someone's property? But it was an alley so the only stuff out there was yard debris or trash to be picked up by the city. There must have been something in that pile. She pulled out from the alley onto the street, thankful that she hadn't blown a tire, but then, feeling guilty, she decided she had to make a quick stop. She grabbed her flashlight and ran back down the alley. She shone her flashlight, sweeping it from side to side. There was a pile of wood, stacked neatly next to some trashcans. Several logs seemed to have toppled off it. That must have been what she'd hit. Relieved, she ran back to her SUV and gunned the engine. Dana would make a song and dance about being late. Thank goodness the SUV was in her name only. If it were joint property, she could only imagine the torrent of criticism that Dana would have hurled when she saw the damage to the body and paintwork.

She was almost at Dana's house. Once her ex had finished dressing her down she'd take Sammy home and put him to bed. Then she'd be able to relive the earlier part of the evening, remembering the way Kat's eyes danced and how a little dimple appeared in her cheek when she smiled. In the morning she'd see what the damage was to the Hyundai and ask her cousin Rico to fix it. And from now on she absolutely wouldn't text while driving. It was stupid and she could have gotten into serious trouble. What if she'd damaged someone's property and they got nasty and wanted to call the cops? An even scarier thought came to mind. What if she'd hit someone and been arrested on the spot? The form she'd completed for her green card had asked her not only if she'd been convicted of a crime, but also if she'd been arrested for one. If she were arrested now, it would be catastrophic. She knew they would repeat that question verbally when she got to her fingerprinting appointment. That appointment next week was so they could do one more full background check. If she told them she'd been arrested that week, even if she were out on bail, they would turn down her request for the ten-year green card. Once they did that, it was the same as being given a deportation notice—she'd have no legal way to stay in the country. How could she have been so stupid as to risk all that?

Just the thought of deportation made her shake all over. People who'd never been through the immigration system had no idea how tenuous life as an "alien" could feel, especially now. It never even occurred to them that people like her, professionals with legal permits, felt some of the same stress and strains as those who lived in the shadows. They didn't realize that until she was actually a citizen, she didn't enjoy the full protections they did. But now, finally, she was getting closer to that day. The ten-year card would end much of that stress, and long before the ten years were up she'd be eligible to apply for citizenship and become just like everyone else.

For months before she got the letter requesting her presence for fingerprinting, she'd visualized herself over and again getting the card. She spent nights picturing herself walking through those wide doors into the Tampa Immigration and Naturalization office, waiting way past her appointment time (as she always did), then getting called back to an office. In her mind, the immigration official who would quiz her and Dana would be supportive and sympathetic and would smile warmly at them when they gave her the stamp of approval. Gordy tried not to remember the officer who granted the two-year card. A large military-looking women who'd made it clear she didn't believe in same-sex marriage, she'd scowled throughout the entire interview and then snarled at Gordy in her Russian-accented English, almost spitting as she made jabbing motions in the air. "You think you citizen? You not. Don't forget. You commit crime? You deported."

At the time she'd shrugged it off. She wasn't going to commit a crime, and there was no reason why an upstanding professional would be deported. She'd felt pretty secure. But lately everything had changed. Just this week a soccer coach had been deported, his only crime being a traffic violation.

She was so close to the finish line, but tonight she'd almost blown it. All she had to do was keep her nose clean for another week. And if that meant picking up her son late and getting in trouble with her ex for not texting, the price was worth it.

CHAPTER SIX

Officer Delgado

The dispatch officer's voice crackled over the intercom.

"Major crime for you to check out tonight, Del." Officer Delgado felt his chest tighten. He didn't want to start dealing with any major crime. That's why he'd joined the Gulfport police force. No murders, nothing violent or grizzly. Especially not on the night shift. Mostly drunks who needed to be transported to St. Anthony's to dry out, or petty robbery from houses where the owners never even locked their doors.

"Go ahead." His tone was gruff.

"I'm joking," she said, and Del felt himself relax. "Barking dogs. 24th and Ohio."

Del nodded, even though the dispatch officer couldn't see him. "I know the one."

Most dog owners were reliable and responsible, but every now and then there were the ones who made you wonder why they had a dog at all. If it was the canine he was thinking of, the large bulldog was constantly escaping his yard and roaming the neighborhood. The dog wasn't dangerous, but it upset the other neighbors, especially the ones who had small dogs vulnerable to attack. This particular animal had never gotten out at night, but he'd check it out. "Bulldog on the loose, right?"

"Not sure. The complainant said he thought there were two dogs barking and they sounded like they were in someone's yard down the street."

"Don't suppose he thought to just go over there and ring the neighbor's doorbell? This is Gulfport, after all."

"Said he would have, but he's in a wheelchair and his caregiver only comes during the day."

Del put away his laptop and inserted the key into the ignition. He maneuvered the cruiser out of the parking lot and made his way over to the street in question. He parked by the house with the bulldog, cut the engine and stepped out of the vehicle. There was no sign of a dog. Then he heard the barking. It wasn't the bulldog's house after all. It came from the back of a house across the street. Why would someone leave their dogs out at this time of night? Had they gone out for the evening and left the animals in the yard? He hoped not, because that might involve calling in Animal Cruelty. This was one of those rare nights when a frost was forecast overnight. No responsible dog owner should be letting their animals out for more than a few minutes, especially not here in Tampa Bay where dogs, like their owners, were more used to nighttime temperatures in the fifties and sixties. Those poor dogs would feel the cold more than animals used to the winter temperatures up north.

He walked up the path to the front door and rang the bell. It was a two-story house, unusual for this neighborhood, which was mostly made up of small bungalows. He stood back a little to see if there were any lights on. Nothing upstairs, but it looked as if there was a light toward the back of the house. He returned to the cruiser, leaned in to pull his flashlight out from the console, and then started walking down the alley. Trash cans were lined up on one side, and on the other he could see a large pile of chopped-up tree branches. As he walked closer, he could hear dogs in a yard behind a fence going berserk. One of them was scrabbling against the fence while it sounded like the other one was jumping up and down.

"It's okay, boys," he called out. "I'll get you safe indoors one way or the other." He hoped his voice sounded soothing, but the dogs kept up their noise. Poor mutts. Whatever was going on with the owner of those animals, he had no sympathy for him or her. He shone the flashlight beam above the woodpile then flicked it over to the other side of the alley. Nothing unusual anywhere. There was a side gate in the fence, just before the pile of branches.

He decided to try to open it, although he was sure it would be locked. He lifted the latch, and surprisingly the gate opened. No sooner was he through than the two dogs took a flying leap past him and darted out into the alley.

He spun around, calling to them. "Come on, boys; it's okay, come to Papa." But they'd already charged past him. Both ran straight to the woodpile.

He trained his flashlight to the pile of branches. This time he saw what he'd missed before. A figure on the ground. A woman. The dogs licked at her face frantically. She mumbled something. A few strides and he was by her side. She lay jammed against the woodpile and he smelled alcohol on her breath. He thought he saw some dried blood on her face. Jeez. Had she been so drunk she'd fallen into the pile of branches?

He knelt beside her and pushed the dogs back a little, trying to lift her to a sitting position. She screamed in pain and he jumped.

"I think I'm injured." Her voice was weak. He looked closer. A slightly older woman, about the same age as his stepmom. She was in pajamas and barefoot. On a night like this. She must have been plastered.

"You tripped?" He tried to mask his scorn.

"No. A car . . ." her voice trailed off. He waited. What could a car have to do with all this?

"Please, call an ambulance," she said. "And I'll need someone to look after my dogs."

That was the thing he hated about drunks. They always felt so entitled, making demands, asking for help, when mostly they were the ones causing all the problems.

"You can't get up?"

"It hurts when I try to move. My arm feels broken." Her breath was labored, but she was trying to tell him more. "The force was so strong."

"What force?"

"From the car." She moaned. "Please . . . an ambulance?"

He shook his head in disgust, but pulled out his radio and put in a call, then turned back to the woman.

"You've been drinking, right?" He shone the flashlight in her eyes. They didn't look bloodshot, but he could smell alcohol on her breath.

"A glass or two of wine, but . . ." Officer Delgado shook his head. Alcoholics never seemed to realize that the police knew to double whatever amount they said they'd imbibed. Forget glasses, she'd probably drained at least one bottle, if not two.

"You better tell me what happened." He wondered if she even remembered.

"Garbage night." She winced as she spoke. "Was putting cans out . . ." She paused for a moment as if talking drained her. "A car came. Out of nowhere. Hit me."

"You were knocked down by a vehicle?"

"Yes. Please . . . it's hard to talk."

Holy cow. If that's what had happened, maybe it had nothing to do with her drinking. *If* that's what happened.

"What kind of car?"

She sighed. "I couldn't see . . . blinded by headlights."

"And after he hit you, the driver didn't stop?"

She tried to shake her head, but winced from pain.

The whole thing sounded far-fetched to him. If she was blinded by the headlights, the driver must have seen her. Maybe it didn't happen like that at all. Maybe she was wandering down the alley trying to sober up and walked right in front of the vehicle.

"They just drove away," he repeated, trying to keep the skepticism out of his voice. '*Barking dogs*,' dispatch had said, and he'd felt relieved. He'd thought he could do a quick neighborhood visit and then get back to the police academy catalog he'd been browsing. Well, the laugh was on him now. The whole damn night was going to be taken up with this. Since her injuries might be serious, he'd have to accompany her to the hospital to find out for sure what they were. After he left the hospital, he'd need to come back to look for evidence—and whatever happened there'd be a ton of paperwork. Goddamn. There went his shift. And then when he got home . . . He sighed.

He wanted to get started with his investigation right away. Rescue would be here pretty soon so he only had a few minutes to get the information he needed from the woman. After that the paramedics would take over and do their job. He tried again.

"What kind of vehicle was it?"

She moaned softly, clutching her head in one hand, while the other arm dangled at her side. "Big," she said. As if that told him anything he needed to know.

"A sedan? A pickup? You must be able to tell me that."

"An SUV?" Her tone was hesitant, as if he knew the answer better than she did.

"OK, good. An SUV. What make? What color?"

"Gray? Silver?" Again the questioning, hesitant tone.

He waited for more. When she didn't give it, he repeated his question. "What make or model?"

She closed her eyes. He put his notepad down. He wasn't going to get any more answers from her. He needed to secure the scene. He had tape in the vehicle but could see there was nothing to attach it to. He had a couple of cones in the trunk that he could place at each end of the alley, though he'd have to move them when Rescue arrived. He stood up.

"Please . . ." The woman looked up at him, terror in her eyes. "Don't leave me!"

"No, Ma'am. I'm right here. Just need to make sure no one else drives down this alley."

She shook her head. "No one will." Her voice was shaky, and he realized she was crying. "They never do."

Which seemed to directly contradict what she said had happened.

He sighed. Since this was his territory, he'd need to start searching for any physical evidence that might be lying around as soon as possible. If he was lucky something would have broken off the vehicle and he could check the serial number. That was the best-case scenario. He'd have to wait until tomorrow to do some door-knocking with the neighbors. After that he could check registration records for silver-gray SUV owners in the neighborhood, but with a description that vague it would be a long shot. If he got lucky it might all come together pretty quickly. If not, it could be the beginning of a long and futile investigation.

Officer Delgado went back to the woman whose name he still didn't know. He'd get all that information when the ambulance came since they'd need it too. He hoped her injuries were serious. Not because he wished her harm, but because if they weren't life-threatening he'd have to do the whole investigation himself. He wouldn't be able to call in detective backup from the county. It would be just him, and if he didn't get results pretty quickly, they'd just let it go. He'd seen it happen plenty of times. The victims were always outraged, but what could he do? He disliked drunks, but he disliked hit-and-run drivers even more. He wanted justice just as much as the victims did, but sometimes his hands were tied.

If only this woman had stayed indoors this evening. He'd taken the night shift so he could study and get ahead. Without his wife working, he needed a pay raise and one way to get it was to keep taking classes. Online courses were ideal for him. At least, they were when his time wasn't taken up with investigations. He just hoped this one would be over quickly.

CHAPTER SEVEN

Kat

Kat rubbed her arms as she jogged her usual route along the waterfront. It was such a pleasure to feel a chill in the air. She was even wearing leggings, which she hardly ever needed to do. She'd barely slept last night. Gordy's news about her upcoming immigration appointment meant that soon she'd be free to marry again. Part of Kat knew that was a crazy thought and that they hadn't known each other nearly long enough to be thinking like that. But another part was pretty convinced that this was love, and it was different from any other emotion she'd had with any other girlfriend. Last night Kat had tried to call Wynn. She wanted to know whether her friend thought she was rushing into things. Surprisingly Wynn hadn't answered or returned her call.

Kat thought back to how they'd met. For months she'd forced herself to research every aspect of running a cafe, from licensing permits to potential recipes, surprising even herself by how diligent she'd been. Her brother, always one to disparage her, would be shocked if he knew how many hours she'd spent reading books and articles about finances, leases, employees and supplies. Then, a few months ago she'd taken the plunge and joined BusNet where she'd met Wynn.

There were about forty attendees at the business networking meeting, three-quarters of whom were men. They ranged in age, but they all looked serious and very intent on pushing their products. Within five minutes of walking through the door, she'd been given business cards by a veterinarian, an electrician, and an attorney. They'd all taken their seats on either sides of long, narrow tables set in a U-shape, and Kat had found herself looking at the woman directly opposite her. She was a skinny older woman with long gray curls and bracelets up and down the length of her arms who appeared very different from the other women in their fitted business dresses and power suits. Kat had worn her usual cargo shorts because it hadn't occurred to her that she ought to dress up for a support group for business owners.

Everyone was given thirty seconds to describe their businesses. Some were glib and practiced, others hesitant, and a few people had made up catchy slogans. The one that had stuck with her was a nursing home "where it looks like home and feels like family."

"In six-months' time I'm going to be the owner and manager of Kat-Kat's Tea Emporium," she told the group with a lot more confidence than she felt. She told them how it was going to happen and added, "It's a big risk. A lot of small businesses fail, especially restaurants. I don't want to be one of them." There had been a few nods and sympathetic smiles, and then there'd been a presentation from a motivational speaker who described how he'd gone from making twenty thousand a year to half a million. Kat couldn't help wondering if it were true. Why would he still be coming to this meeting if he were doing so well?

Afterward, the interesting-looking woman with the bangles and curly gray hair, who turned out to be Wynn, had sought her out. "If there's any way I can help you, just let me know. My jewelry-making business is going better than I ever dreamed it would, and while some of that is due to my brilliant daughter teaching me everything I need to know about online marketing, I've also learned a lot of my own lessons along the way. I'll be happy to share them with you."

After that they sat next to each other every week, chatting before and after the meetings. Wynn described her kids and her business, but she never mentioned a husband. Eventually Kat decided to take the plunge and ask.

"Husband?" Wynn's eyebrows had shot up in surprise. "Don't you recognize a sister when you see one?" Kat had been embarrassed, but Wynn had smiled. "What do you think happens to young femmes when they get older?"

That was three months ago, and since then they'd established a comfortable friendship that included going out for coffee after the networking meetings and sharing problems on the phone. Kat liked that Wynn didn't text. She'd almost forgotten what it was like to curl up on the sofa or sprawl across a deck-chair while indulging in a good old-fashioned phone chat. At first their conversations had been mostly business, but lately they'd become more personal. Wynn talked about her daughters, but seemed reticent when talking about her love life, past or present. But then again, while Kat had babbled on about Gordy, she hadn't exactly been forthcoming about her previous relationship fiasco.

Kat thought about Wynn's warning to take things slowly with Gordy. Was she right? Was Kat moving too quickly? It was ironic that she was moving so fast in romance, but so slowly in business. Everyone was telling her she needed to stop procrastinating, and they had a point. She'd heard about a possible location just off the main drag that could be perfect for Kit-Kat's. Maybe today she'd call that property manager and get details. No, she told herself as she slowed down her running so she could start her cooldown. Not maybe. Definitely. She'd commit to calling that property manager today.

Kat turned the corner and ran up the steps to her apartment. She was unlacing her running shoes when the phone rang.

"Kat?" The voice was familiar, but she couldn't place it. "It's Michaela, Wynn's daughter."

Her stomach lurched. Wynn hadn't returned her call from the previous night. If Mikki was calling it must mean bad news.

"Is she okay?"

"Not—not exactly." She heard Mikki's voice catch, and waited. "There was an accident, a hit-and-run. She's in the hospital."

"Oh my god."

"I can give you all the details when I see you, but for right now, would you be willing to go over to her house and take care of the dogs?"

"Take care . . . ?"

"Run them around the block and feed them. Tina's already driving down, and I'll get a flight as soon as I can, so we'll take over after that. Also, there's a couple of things I think Mom should have at the hospital. Could you pick them up and take them over there? "

"I don't have a key."

"I'll tell you where it is. Mom's still naive enough to leave one in a simple place outside. I know, it's crazy, but she does."

"Not crazy at all. This is Gulfport. I'll guarantee every other house has a key under the mat or hidden in a planter by the front door." She scribbled down the list Wynn's daughter gave her, along with the hospital details.

"If you can get there as soon as possible, that would be great. I know she'd like to have someone with her until we arrive."

Kat sighed. She'd had plans for today, but of course none of that mattered now. She grabbed her phone and headed out the door.

The key was where Michaela said it would be. The minute she put it in the lock, the dogs started barking. Moments later, Queen barreled into Kat's chest, while Latifah started jumping up and down like a jack-in-the-box. Kat ran through the house, past the mudroom and opened up the back door. The dogs shoved past her and flung themselves onto the grass where they both did what she'd hoped they would. She left them out there while she opened and closed kitchen cupboards looking for their dog food. She had no idea how much they usually got, but decided that the important thing was simply to feed them. She poured large bowlfuls of kibble, put them on the floor and opened the back door.

While the dogs were eating, Kat searched for Wynn's cell phone. She had no idea where it might be. Wynn was like an absentminded professor who was as likely to leave her phone in the freezer as she was to put it somewhere obvious like the kitchen table. There were piles of magazines scattered on the sofa, but pushing them aside revealed nothing. Several bags of dog treats sat on the dining room table, but no phone. The counter top was surprisingly tidy with an assortment of plates and dishes stacked next to the kitchen sink. Still no phone.

Kat made her way upstairs to the bedroom and was relieved to spot Wynn's phone on the nightstand, along with an empty wine bottle and a half-full glass of red wine. Once she had the phone, she gathered up the toiletries Mikki had requested. She wondered what kind of injuries Wynn had sustained, but if she wanted her phone and toothbrush, things couldn't be too bad.

As she let herself out of the front door, she noticed a large silver SUV driving down the alley. It was going slowly and it paused outside Wynn's back-gate. Kat figured the driver was looking for treasures—today was trash day. It was amazing what kinds of things you could find from trash-picking. Kat had several items in her home, including both her end-tables, that she'd found on the street. She watched as the man walked over to the pile of wood stacked by the side of the house and bent over it, peering as if he'd lost something. If they were up north, she could imagine him piling it into the back of his vehicle for firewood, but nobody had wood fires in Gulfport. After a few minutes he straightened up, swept his gaze up and down the alley, then climbed back into his car. Odd, he hadn't even looked at the rocking chair someone had put out on the other side of the alley.

Kat pulled open the door of the old Ford pickup she'd recently acquired, threw Wynn's stuff on the passenger seat and drove away.

CHAPTER EIGHT

Wynn

A man was trying to talk to her.

"Would you like the good news first, or the bad news?"

For a moment she had no idea where she was and who the male voice could possibly belong to. She struggled into consciousness, pulling herself out of a deep fog. She became aware that she was lying in bed, but not her own. It felt as if she were in some sort of straitjacket with her arms positioned in front of her. She forced her eyes to open, and through the fog she saw the outline of someone standing above her. She blinked and tried to focus her vision.

A doctor. She moved her eyes and saw blinking machines and an IV pole. A hospital. Suddenly it all started to flood back into her mind. Putting the trash out. Vehicle headlights. A loud noise. Pain. She snapped her eyes a few times and felt suddenly alert. How long had she been here? She couldn't afford to spend time in a hospital—she had to get home and back to work as soon as possible. What if one of her daughters called and she didn't answer? They'd start worrying. She tried to sit up and pain shot through her.

"Please, don't try to move."

The doctor talking to her was a ridiculously young man who looked more like a high school student than a hospital trauma physician. She could have sworn the shadow on his unshaven chin was merely peach fuzz.

"I have lots of information for you, but I like to give my patients some control. So, you want the good news first?" His voice sounded cheerful and perky as if she had played the lottery and the only issue was whether she'd won a small fortune or a large one.

She tried to nod her head, but even that hurt and made her nauseous. "Sure." Her mouth felt dry.

"None of your injuries is life-threatening and in six months you'll be as good as new."

"Six months?" Wynn breathed heavily, aware of how painful it was. "Surely that's the bad news."

"I don't mean it will take that long to feel better. That's going to happen in a couple of days."

Wynn felt frustration rising in her. There was a big difference between a few days and several months. Why couldn't this young man just say what he meant?

"You have some injuries that will heal pretty quickly, and a few that will take a little longer."

"What's going on with my arms?" Now that her eyes were open, Wynn could see some sort of metal contraption encircling her right forearm. It appeared to be attached to her though she had no idea how. The lower part of her left arm was encased in white plaster.

"You fractured your left wrist."

Wynn felt an enormous wave of relief flow through her body. Her left wrist only! Maybe there was a way she could still get some of her work done. It wouldn't be easy to manipulate the pieces with only one hand, but it wouldn't be impossible, especially if she hired an assistant to hold things for her.

"You also broke your right arm."

"No, please . . ." Wynn groaned. "Are you sure?"

The physician nodded. "No baseball for you for a while." He grinned, pleased with himself. Did he think that hands and arms were only important to young people or athletes?

"I make jewelry for a living. There's nothing to joke about. If I can't use my right hand, I can't work."

The doctor looked momentarily taken aback. "Please don't worry about that now. We've already realigned some bone fragments and I'll talk to you more later about what comes next.

You have some other injuries I need to discuss with you." This, Wynn suspected, was the bad news. "The reason moving was so painful for you last night was because you broke your hip."

Damn. She was going to be way more incapacitated than she'd realized.

"It doesn't hurt as much as it did last night."

"That's because we fixed it already."

Wynn was so tired she could barely understand what he was saying.

"Are you saying I've already had surgery?"

"Yes. Once we knew you were stable, we needed to get that hip done as soon as possible, and you were in luck because we had a surgeon in the OR who's a hip expert. Given your age, he decided to do a total hip replacement." Her age? Had he really just implied she was a doddering ninety-year-old instead of a vibrant woman in her early sixties? She closed her eyes. Make it all go away. Please, just make it all disappear.

Doogie Howser apparently wasn't to be stopped. "You have some internal injuries too."

The arms and hips weren't enough? She wanted to scream. It wasn't fair. She couldn't deal with all this. It was too much. She wouldn't listen. If she could have closed her ears, she would have. Instead, she closed her eyes, as if that would somehow block out the doctor's words. Hopefully it would signal that she was done with him for now. She heard rustling and then a familiar voice, not her doctor's.

"Wynn?"

She opened her eyes. "Kat!" She was so glad to see her that for a moment she forgot how awful everything was.

Kat moved over to the bed and leaned forward, as if she were looking to hold her hand.

"You better not touch me. I'm broken all over. Right, doc?" She snorted.

The doctor turned to Kat. "Your mom has some external injuries that I've already informed her of. Broken wrist, arm, and hip."

"My mom?" Kat's eyebrows had shot upward. "You think I'm Wynn's daughter?"

The doctor looked rattled. "I made an assumption. May I ask how you're related?"

"She's my friend." Wynn said. She had no use for this brash young man, so full of himself and so lacking any kind of bedside manner.

"I was about to inform you of your internal injuries. Would you like your friend to stay or leave?" He paused a little before he said the word friend, and Wynn figured he thought she'd used a euphemism for partner. Let him think it. Kat was cute. Nothing wrong with him thinking his patient was a cradle-snatcher.

"Last night we did a CT scan to evaluate potential trauma to your abdomen. You have an injured spleen."

Wynn sighed. "I don't even know what a spleen is."

"It's in the upper far left part of your abdomen and it acts as a filter for blood as part of your immune system. You have a subcapsular hematoma, bleeding that's contained in the capsule surrounding the spleen. As the capsule doesn't stretch indefinitely, it often stops the bleeding by elevating the pressure in the spleen." Wynn felt herself drifting away. What on earth was he talking about? Did he really think she could follow any of this? She closed her eyes.

"Can you just explain things in plain English?" Kat said, a hint of impatience in her voice. Wynn was so glad she was there.

"A hematoma can rupture anytime. Luckily we didn't have to remove the spleen, which would have put your friend's immune system at risk. We'll be keeping a close eye on her to ensure she doesn't start any additional bleeding."

Wynn opened her eyes. "Is that what's making it so hard to breathe?"

"No. You've also got some broken ribs. One of them lacerated your lung."

Wynn felt tears pricking behind her eyes. The enormity of her situation felt suddenly overwhelming.

"It's too much . . ." She tried to talk, then burst into tears. Despite everything, she wished Barker were here. It had been almost four years but still she had moments when all she wanted was Barker at her side. Barker had always taken charge and known what to do. Except when she hadn't.

Wynn wanted to brush away her tears, then realized she couldn't even do that.

"It's okay." Kat laid her hand gently on Wynn's arm. "You have friends. And your daughters are both coming home. They can look after you."

"No." Her voice was weak. "I don't want them to miss school. Tell them not to come."

"It's too late. They're already on their way. Don't worry, between us we'll sort everything out. As the doctor said, the only thing you have to do is concentrate on getting well."

Doogie started talking to her about surgeries and casts and walkers, but she let the words wash over her. What did it matter? She was going to be stuck in the hospital for goodness-knows-how-long and after that she'd be imprisoned at home. She was in pain and that was likely to continue for quite some time. She wouldn't be able to work and she'd be riddled with debt for years. Not only was her business going to be ruined, but who knew how much of all this her insurance would cover? She'd probably need to pay thousands of dollars before it even kicked in. Money that she didn't have.

The doctor was still talking, and whenever he paused and looked at her questioningly she nodded, which seemed to be what he wanted. She'd ask Kat later to tell her what he said and what she'd agreed to. Meanwhile she had to figure out how she was going to deal with all this. There was no way she'd let her daughters come home to look after her. It wasn't fair to them, after all the work they'd put in just to get where they were.

It didn't sound like she'd be able to manage by herself, but she couldn't afford to hire a caregiver. Not unless she could find some way to pay for one. It was screwed up. She shouldn't have to pay for something that wasn't her fault. The damn driver who knocked her down, that's who should pay. Yes, the driver! That bastard must have auto insurance. Last night when that cop had asked her questions about what had happened, she hadn't understood why he was asking such specific details. But now she did. She had to make sure they caught the fucker.

Wynn was in pain and exhausted. But she knew one thing. That driver was damn well going to pay, and not just financially. He'd hit her and hadn't even stopped to come to her aid. She was pretty sure that was called a hit-and-run and that someone could be arrested for that.

Wynn knew what it was like to be arrested. She was going to make damn sure the hit-and-run driver did too.

CHAPTER NINE

Gabriella

Gordy stood at the bus stop, waiting for the bus to appear. It had been so long since she'd had to use public transportation that she didn't even know if she needed to have the exact fare or how much it was. When she'd first come to the States, she'd depended on buses and trains, but that was in a city where public transportation was readily available, frequent and reliable. When she moved to this part of Florida, she discovered that if you didn't have a car, you were doomed. Sometimes when she mapped places she needed to get to, her GPS would show her how long it would take by public transportation: a twenty-minute car trip could easily take three hours. She'd been so thankful she had her car.

An old man shuffled up to the stop and stood by her, holding on to the bus signpost. There was no seat or bench for him to rest on, nor any shelter. What did people do in the middle of the day when the sun was blazing down on them? Gracias a Dios she had her own vehicle, at least she did when she wasn't doing stupid things like texting and driving. She dreaded to think how much the repair was going to cost, but it served her right. What if her son had been in the car with her?

Sammy had grumbled when she told him they'd have to walk to school. She'd offered to carry his lunch box and had tucked it awkwardly under her arm while she held him tight with her other hand.

"It's too far," Sammy whined as they walked. "Can't we get a taxi?"

She smiled to herself. What did her child know of poverty? Nothing. And she was glad of it. Still, maybe she'd been overprotective of him. He ought to be able to walk a few blocks without thinking he deserved help.

"Here, you carry this." She thrust the SpongeBob SquarePants lunch box at him. He pouted as he took it from her. Maybe from now on she'd make him walk to school on a regular basis, or at least on those days when he didn't have some unwieldy art project that needed carrying. Sammy loved creating things with his hands. He'd started with Legos when he was barely two. In kindergarten, while other children scribbled indecipherable messes on construction paper, dashing the crayons back and forth as if they were model racing cars, Sammy had created his first picture, green grass dotted with red, yellow, and orange wildflowers.

"It's our garden, Mama," he'd said proudly, holding the picture up for Gordy to admire after Dana had picked him up from school. Dana had winked at Gordy, as if to imply that it was just a bunch of scribbles, but Gordy really could see the grass and the garden. Dana always was the impatient one.

Last night, Dana had sighed and shaken her head from side to side when Gordy had finally pulled up outside her house. By then the bumper was scraping across the pavement and the headlights were no longer pointing in the direction they were meant to.

"So that's why you didn't make it on time." She'd walked around the SUV, examining it carefully. "I knew there had to be some good reason. Even *you* wouldn't mess up where Sammy's concerned." The implied criticism was mild, but Gordy decided not to mention that the accident had happened after she was already running late. Dana had invited her in and made her a cup of hot chocolate, fussing over her and even offering a suggestion for a car mechanic. When she woke Sammy up and carried him out to the car, she told their son to be a good boy.

"Mommy G's had a shock, Mamita, sé buena. Be good."

Gordy was surprised to hear Dana repeat to Sammy the Spanish words she'd heard so many times over the years. Were things finally going to settle down between her and Dana?

"Excuse me," Gordy turned to the man clutching the bus stop for support. "How much is the bus fare?"

He looked at her and frowned.

"You don't know?" She urged. Surely he had to know. He shrugged his shoulders, then pulled something out of his pocket and showed it to her. A plastic card with a picture of a beach and the word "Go" on it. Of course he had no idea. He had a monthly bus pass. He was about to shove it back in his pocket but stopped. She looked up and saw the bus approaching. She scrambled for her wallet and pulled out a handful of bills and coins, ready for whatever amount she might need.

"Wait!" She heard someone behind her, and saw a thin dark-skinned woman, her hair still in pink curlers, pulling two toddlers whose feet barely touched the ground as the woman ran toward the bus stop.

Gordy climbed on to the bus, saw the sign that told her the fare was $2.25, then took her time sorting out the fare, glad to delay the bus long enough for the woman and kids. As she found a seat she felt grateful she'd never had to navigate buses while carrying a child and shopping. Sammy was definitely spoiled, but after all they'd planned it that way. Gordy would have tried for kids the moment they both knew their relationship was headed in that direction but Dana wanted to ensure they had enough money, not just to pay for sperm, but to cover all the ongoing expenses having a child would entail. Gordy looked out of the window at the passing scenery, but what she saw was that magical night when she lay on their king-size bed, her butt resting on a pile of quilted pillows, her pelvis tilted upward. Mercedes Sosa was crooning softly in the background as Dana knelt between her legs, and carefully squirted the vial of sperm inside her. Neither of them had expected it to work the very first time, but as Dana liked to point out, "When did you ever see me fail when I set my mind to something?"

The following year it was Gordy kneeling between Dana's legs, month after month, but nothing happened. Dana made it clear the blame was on Gordy for not being the expert inseminator, dismissing the possibility that her body wasn't receptive to the rushing liquid. Eventually she gave in and had a doctor inseminate her but the result was the same. Which was a relief really, because by then it was clear to Gordy that bringing a second child into their family wouldn't be a good idea.

As the bus left Gulfport and headed to St. Petersburg, Gordy realized that it was rather a pleasure not driving. She could let her mind wander wherever it wanted to, without the stress of dealing with traffic lights and impatient drivers. Where her mind wanted to wander was to what had happened before she rammed her car into the woodpile, to that very delectable woman who, despite having no dress sense and no rhythm when she danced, made Gordy's heart skip. Were things really going to work out? Could she let herself believe that this relationship was going to be different than the one with Dana? Things were moving so quickly. Part of her felt it was right, and part of her still wasn't sure. Because of Sammy she couldn't afford to make any mistakes. But how would she know what Kat was like with kids if she didn't introduce them?

She decided it was time to take the plunge. The next time she saw Kat, she'd suggest an outing with Sammy. Just something low-key where she'd introduce Kat as a new friend. Maybe they'd go to the Great Explorations museum, over in St. Pete. Sammy loved building things with the architectural blocks and the Lego accessories they didn't have at home. And there was a kitchen area they'd never explored so maybe Kat could do that with him.

Gordy sat back and looked out of the window as the bus crawled through town. Despite messing up her SUV last night, she had to admit that, all in all, life was pretty good.

CHAPTER TEN

Gabriella

Gordy was shocked at how long it took her to get to work. Ten minutes in the car turned out to be thirty on the bus, followed by a fifteen-minute walk to Pelican Manor. The CNAs would have been in trouble for being that late, but luckily she made her own hours.

She walked up the sweeping driveway and buzzed herself in through the front door. The nursing director, Mandy, looked surprised to see her coming in that way, instead of from the parking lot at the rear of the facility.

"Car trouble," Gordy explained. "I had to take the bus."

"Say no more," Mandy said, a look of sympathy in her eyes. "Mr. Basanti's been asking for you."

"I saw him yesterday. It's great that he holds on to who I am. Now if only he could remember that he's already talked to me this week, that would be even better!"

"At least he enjoys seeing you," Mandy said. "I still can't get Mrs. Campbell to agree to talk to you. And she needs it a lot more than some of the others. The overnight worker had to go into her room again last night. Mrs. C. was having nightmares, screaming at the top of her lungs. And when the worker went in, Mrs. C. just cowered in the corner, like she was ready to be assaulted."

"It's hard. So many old people grew up with the idea that you should keep your troubles to yourself. I'm sure the only reason Mr.

Basanti likes talking to me is because he thinks I'm a friend of his daughter. If he remembered that I was a psychologist, he'd probably run a mile."

Gordy walked through Mandy's office to her own little cubbyhole. She liked this facility. She split her time between Pelican Manor and Glendale Court. At Glendale, there was nowhere to meet with clients, and often she found herself perched on the edge of a bed in someone's room while they talked.

"Isn't it a waste of time?" Dana had asked when Gordy took the job. "What good is counseling old people in their 80s and 90s some of whom don't even remember you from week to week? I mean, you're getting paid, which is the important thing, but won't Medicare catch on at some point that this is a scam?"

She was wrong. It wasn't a scam at all. People didn't stop having feelings and emotions when they got older. In fact, for many of her clients, life was harder than it had been when they were young. None of them had aspired to live in a nursing home or assisted living facility when they got old. Most of them had had careers and jobs, houses and families where they called the shots, at least as much as anyone else. Now, sometimes the only things they had control over was whether to have chicken or pasta for lunch, and even that was only in the homes where they were offered a choice. These men and women had been fit and active and had thought nothing of jumping into the car when they needed to run errands or go shopping. They hadn't expected their bodies to let them down, leaving them incontinent, shuffling around with the aid of a walker, or confined to a wheelchair. Her friend Dev, a paraplegic, always said, "I'm not confined to a wheelchair; I'm liberated by one." But she was young and the wheelchair did indeed bring her freedom. For people who'd been able-bodied all their lives, not being able to walk didn't feel liberating at all. And on top of everything, most of Gordy's clients had lost all the people who'd been most important in their lives—parents, siblings, spouses, and often children too. Why did Dana think they didn't need to process all that?

Gordy walked down the hallway and knocked on the door of one of her clients.

"Mr. Dawson?" She knocked again. "Are you there?" She didn't like to yell, but Mr. Dawson insisted there was nothing wrong with his hearing and refused to wear aids. Other clients would tell her to just come in if they didn't respond, but Mr. Dawson always looked completely shocked when she walked in uninvited.

A nurse's aide came running down the hall. "Didn't they tell you? He's in the hospital again. The usual." Mr. Dawson's life was a balancing act of trying to ensure enough fluid to keep his kidneys going, but not so much that it made his congestive heart failure worse.

Gordy went back to her office. She was glad for the respite. She pulled her phone out of her briefcase and dialed her cousin to ask about her car.

"How bad is it?" she asked

"Nothing I can't handle. It'll probably take me two or three days. There are parts I'll need to order. Are you going to make an insurance claim?"

"I don't think so. Let's wait and see how much the total cost is going to be."

"It doesn't work like that, Cuz. You have to decide right away. If you're going to use insurance, the adjuster has to approve all the work I'm going to do. Once I start fixing it, it's too late to start a claim."

"I didn't realize . . . in all the years I've been driving, I've never once had an accident." Gordy sat down at her desk and pulled out her laptop, ready to look up whatever information she might need if she were going to file a claim. "What do you think I should do?"

Her cousin paused. "As soon as you make a claim, they'll double your premiums. Especially since it was your fault. They might even drop your insurance altogether. Normally I'd want my customer to claim on their insurance, but for you . . . I can get some of the parts secondhand and if I do most of the work myself I won't have to charge you labor."

Gordy closed the laptop back up. "That would be great. But don't lose money on me. I'm willing to pay what I have to."

"I know. It won't be cheap, but I'll do the best I can."

"Don't forget, my car's still registered to my old address."

Gordy put the phone away and headed down the corridor to her next patient. She loved doing direct client service. Ironic to think that if her job at the university hadn't been defunded she would probably have stayed in research for ever.

CHAPTER ELEVEN

Wynn

Wynn was trying in vain to find a comfortable position for herself. Everything hurt, inside and out. She looked up at the TV screen, completely uninterested in what was on it, but wishing she could use it to distract herself. Just when she'd decided that she couldn't bear daytime TV, the door was flung open and Michaela burst through it.

She came forward then stopped, her eyes widening as she took in the contraptions attached to Wynn. "Oh my God, Mom!"

"It's not as bad as it looks," Wynn said, even though in actuality it was worse. She gave as much of a smile as she could muster. She couldn't help noticing that even though Michaela had presumably been up since dawn and rushing around airports, she looked her usual perfectly coiffed self, her wavy long hair pulled back neatly, her shirt crisp and her pants pressed.

A moment later the door opened again and Wynn's second daughter appeared.

"Hi, Kallie."

"Mom!" The tone was scolding.

"Sorry, honey. Tina. I'm on painkillers and don't know what I'm saying." Once the adoption for both girls was finalized, Kallie had asked if she could go by her middle name, Tina. Wynn wasn't sure it was a good idea, but Kallie was determined to distance herself from the life she'd led before the adoption. She said that since Tina was also the name of her sports heroine, Martina Navratilova, it would be a daily inspiration to her. Wynn smiled to herself now, noting that Tina was also her usual self, only in her case that meant she looked as if she had just got out of bed. She was dressed in baggy pants that looked more like pajamas and her hair ricocheted in every different direction. People who didn't know the girls were adopted and not blood sisters often wondered how Wynn could have two such different-looking daughters.

Both girls approached the bedside.

"What were you doing out that late?" Tina's voice was accusatory. Wynn grimaced inwardly. Wasn't it the parent who was meant to ask the child that question?

"Who did this?" Mikki sounded angry.

"Your Mom isn't up to long explanations right now." A nurse had come into the room unnoticed and glared at the girls as she checked Wynn's IV.

"I'm always glad to see you, but there was no need for you to come." Wynn told them. "Stay at the house tonight, but I want you both to go back to school tomorrow."

Both girls shook their heads. "No way. You've been there for us, and now we're going to be there for you."

"I'm not going to argue with you about it."

"That's right, you're not." Tina stood with both hands on her hips. "I'm going to talk to your doctors and find out exactly what's going on, and then the three of us will make decisions together."

Wynn couldn't help smiling to herself. While Mikki had been only too happy to embrace being parented at age sixteen when the adoptions were finalized, Tina had remained the independent soul the foster care system had forced her to be. Those last two years of high school Wynn had needed to pull rank as the adult in the home, but now that Tina was legally an adult, it wasn't going to be as easy. She was pretty sure Mikki would agree to return to school right away, but Tina would be a harder sell.

Mikki pulled up a chair, while Tina paced back and forth, staring out of the window and glancing at her mom, her expression a mix of frustration and sadness. "We're going to find out who did this," she muttered.

An older man in a white coat entered the room and introduced himself as an orthopedic surgeon.

"I know my colleagues threw a lot of information at you

earlier. Did you have any questions for me?"

Wynn shook her head. She had no idea what they'd told her. She'd meant to ask Kat before she left, but had drifted into sleep and when she awoke, Kat was gone. It seemed as if all day professionals in white coats had told her what was going to happen next, but for the life of her she couldn't remember. She only knew everything was going to be a long drawn-out process.

"Are Mom's arms going to be okay?" Mikki asked.

The doctor turned to her. "Well, as she knows, we're going to have to do surgery," he said. His voice sounded almost gleeful.

"Today?"

"No. We like to recommend waiting until the swelling has gone down before having surgery. She'll just need to keep her arms immobilized and elevated for several days. That will decrease the swelling and give the skin that's been stretched a chance to recover. She's got a lot of cuts and scratches on her arms and we want them to heal a little so they don't get infected"

Mikki and Tina exchanged glances.

"What's with the cast and iron thingy?"

"We're keeping your Mom's arms stable. We've already reduced the bone fragments."

"Reduced . . . ?"

"Sorry. It's just a technical term we use. Means the same as realign." *Then why didn't you say so?* Wynn thought. Usually she had patience for everyone, but right now she was feeling beyond impatient. The doctor turned to Mikki, and even through her haze Wynn noticed how he instantly became a little more charming and deferential. People were always bowled over by her beauty. "Hopefully, your mom won't be in a cast more than six to eight weeks, although with older patients, we never know how long it might take."

Two months? That was a lifetime to an independent jeweler. And had he really just switched to the third person as if she were no longer there? No point in getting upset about that when her whole life was ruined. Let him talk to them. She'd just go back to sleep.

The doctor turned away. "I'll leave you for now. Try to rest and relax," he said.

Rest and relax? Did this playboy have any idea how she was meant to do that? Her business was ruined, her body was shattered, and she was supposed to be calm and take it easy? She closed her eyes and turned her head to the wall. She wanted to go to sleep and never wake up. She could feel herself dozing off.

"Ms. Larimer?"

She had no idea how long she'd been sleeping but the voice wasn't the doctor she'd just been talking to. She opened her eyes. A uniformed officer was standing by her bed, and she realized it must be the one who'd come to her rescue the night before. She looked around for Mikki and Tina. At first she couldn't see them, but when she looked past the cop, she could see them in the hallway talking to some white coats.

"I'm Officer Delgado. Do you remember meeting me yesterday?"

She nodded her head.

"I wanted to see how you're doing and also to see if maybe you could give me any more assistance in solving your case."

"I'm glad you're here." She was shocked at how pitiful her voice sounded, like a nursing home patient who'd lost her teeth. She coughed and tried to clear her throat. "You have to find him."

"I intend to. I have some very serious charges to lay on him when I do. A hit-and-run is a felony offense. He's lucky you're going to survive with no serious injuries."

"No serious ... have you spoken to the doctors?"

He nodded. "I apologize. I know your injuries are serious to you. I meant that they're not life-threatening. At least, they shouldn't be. Broken bones are a pain—literally—but the injuries the police are more concerned with are your internal ones. And I gather they're under pretty good control."

What was with these men? First the doctor and now the officer had implied that what she was going through was just some run-of-the-mill accident. She sighed. She supposed to them it was. And why were the police interested in internal injuries? Was it a polite way of saying they couldn't help her if she'd lost her mind?

"I know I wasn't helpful with the vehicle description," she said. "I'm no expert on cars. But if you could bring me some pictures, I think I might be able to pick out which one it was."

"Good." Officer Delgado had a slight frown, which concerned her.

"You will try to track them down, right?"

He nodded. "Of course. We're a small police force and, since the incident happened in my zone, I'm the investigating officer. But time is of the essence. I'll be back as soon as I can with some images for you to look at. If you can figure out the make and model, it will make my life a heck of a lot easier. Assuming the driver lives somewhere in the area—and since you said folks don't generally drive down your alley, I'm thinking he does—I can track down his registration. I'll be talking to your neighbors, and I'll take another close look at the scene where it happened. I didn't find anything last night, but it's always harder in the dark. Don't you worry Ms. Larimer, we'll get the guy. You just lie back and try to get better."

Wynn wanted to believe him. He sounded as if he were going to do all he could to help her. But ever since The Incident, the term she used in her mind for what had happened four years ago, she had a hard time believing people. The image of being marched down the garden path and into a police cruiser was never far from her mind. And she definitely didn't want to begin thinking about everything that happened after that. She was such a trusting person back then. Things were different now. She steered clear of law enforcement and made people earn her trust. Could she really believe that Officer Delgado was looking out for her?

CHAPTER TWELVE

Wynn

"I'm not going back to school this semester." Tina stood in front of the bed, both hands on her hips, ready for battle.

Wynn sighed. "Let's not talk about this now. It's too early." Everything hurt. In the morning, they'd given her painkillers but she didn't want to be dopey in front of her daughters so she asked to keep them to a minimum. Now she felt her arm throbbing, her back aching.

"I won't change my mind. I'm putting everything into place so that when you come home, I'll be there to take care of you." Tina jutted her chin forward and up a little. She expected to get her way.

Wynn shook her head and felt a shot of pain rip across her cheeks. With all her other injuries, she'd forgotten how bruised her face got when she was knocked over. "Not an option."

Tina pouted. Mikki put her hand on Tina's arm.

"I told her you wouldn't agree to it; otherwise, I'd have offered as well."

Tina shook Mikki's hand off her arm. Mikki moved to the plastic chair by the bed and plonked herself down in it.

"I know you would, honey, and I appreciate it. But we don't need to talk about it right now. They said I'm going to be in here for days, maybe even a couple of weeks. By then you'll both be back at your studies and I'll have a social worker help me figure out how to manage."

She said it with a confidence she didn't feel. In truth, she had no idea how she would be able to go home. But she was the mom and it was her job to protect her children. Especially these two who'd already endured so much.

"I need to sleep now, girls. Why don't you go home and take care of yourselves and the dogs?" She closed her eyes, as if she were dozing off and sensed the girls leaving the room.

After they left, Wynn felt fat tears sliding down her cheeks. Everything hurt, and it wasn't just physical. She ached for herself and for the girls. It hadn't been easy at first. They'd decided as a family to move down to Gulfport, agreeing that a new start was a good idea. With the assistance of her tech-savvy teenage daughters, Wynn had built up her jewelry business into a thriving enterprise. The girls had worked hard both in school and on the tennis courts, and as a result they'd both obtained scholarships to college. Now Tina was willing to give up the dream, and Wynn didn't know if she'd have the strength to resist her. If she were completely honest with herself, she knew that a large part of her wanted Tina to nurse her through her recovery. She couldn't bear the idea of having strangers in her home, helping her with her most basic functioning. But how could she take Tina's future away, or ask her to put it on hold?

It wasn't fair. Everything had been on track. She'd been so proud of her daughters when they went off to college. Last semester, her first without them, she'd wanted so badly to pick up the phone and say, "Come home! I can't bear it without you." She'd had to force herself not to text Tina when she didn't hear from her for days at a time, and to live for Mikki's long rambling phone calls. This second semester she'd started with a better frame of mind. She focused on herself and her new plan to get organized. The night of the accident she'd been so proud that she'd managed to schedule everything so that all she had to do was take out her trash, go to bed, and wake up the next morning ready to spend the entire day completing orders.

And then some idiot had driven down her alley, and in a few seconds he'd ripped away everything.

She lay in the uncomfortable hospital bed and sobbed, her tears increasing with the powerlessness she felt that she couldn't even wipe them away. She wanted to kick and punch with frustration, but she had to keep her body immobile. She wanted to scream, but in a hospital screaming could get you in trouble.

"You up for a visitor?"

Wynn opened her eyes. Donte, her next-door neighbor was standing by her bedside.

"The girls tol' me what happened. Don't reckon I can do nothin' to help." Donte wasn't exactly a friend, but he was much more than a neighbor. He trimmed her trees and did electrical work every time yet another problem surfaced in her house. He'd told her the house needed rewiring, but she couldn't afford it. So he patched things together for her, and in return she portioned out meals she cooked and took them over to him. The first time she invited him for dinner she learned that he wasn't one for socializing. "I get treated for PTSD at the VA," he said, as if that were an obvious reason to refuse the invitation. But he never refused her offers to take home curries and casseroles. She knew it must have been a huge effort for him to come to the hospital.

She thought quickly, needing to come up with something for him. "I need to make some calls," she replied, "and I can't even hold the phone. Will you hold it for me?"

He pushed his gnarled brown hand forward, picked up the cell phone, and held it in front of her. She asked him to flip through her contacts.

"First of all my homeowners insurance. Since this happened outside my house, I'm hoping they can help with expenses."

He dialed and followed the menu instructions until he landed with a live person.

"Name?" The tinny voice at the other end sounded bored.

"Can I ask some questions first? I need to see whether I'm even covered for—"

"I won't know that without your name, will I?" The bored voice now sounded irritated as well. Wynn answered a series of questions as requested, then explained what happened.

"So, it didn't happen inside your home?"

"No, but—"

"Or anywhere on your property."

"No. I just thought . . ."

"What about your employer? Have you checked what they're going to cover for you?"

"I don't have an employer. I work from home."

There was a pause on the other end of the line. Donte started shaking his head, but Wynn didn't know why.

"You mean you telecommute?"

"No. I have a small jewelry business. That's part of why I need all the help I can get from my insurance. I'm not going to be able to create my jewelry for a while and—"

With his free hand, Donte drew a line across his neck, as if he were slitting his throat. Wynn smiled, but still didn't know what he was getting at.

"Let me get this straight. You run a jewelry business out of your home?"

"Oh, no. Nothing like that. I don't sell jewelry, I create it."

"So you're employed by a company. What's the name of the company?"

Donte clicked on the mute button. "Don't be answering them questions. She trying a trick you. Your employment ain't got nothin' to do with it." He unclicked the mute button.

Wynn made her voice sound as professional as possible. "I'm sorry, but I don't see why you're asking me all these questions about my work. I'm calling you because you insure my home, not my work."

"That's fine, Ma'am, but who insures your work?"

"Again, I don't see what the relevance of this is."

"Seems to me you're using your home as a business. If that's the case, your entire policy is null and void. I'm trying to clarify if that's the case."

Wynn gulped and looked at Donte, trying with her eyes to get him to put the phone on mute.

"What shall I say?" She whispered.

He shook his head. "Dunno," he mouthed back.

"Ma'am?" The voice at the other end of the phone no longer sounded bored. It sounded like someone who was hoping to earn a bonus for a job well done.

"I'm sorry," Wynn said. "But I think you've misunderstood this entire conversation. My doctor just came in, so I'm going to have to hang up and call back later, when I can straighten all this out." She would start over with the next person and make sure not to make the same mistake.

"No problem. I've attached a note to your file. Here's your

case number." Wynn shook her head at Donte who was fishing around for a pen and mouthed to him to hang up.

"Honey, I'm sorry," Donte said, replacing the phone by the bedside. "Guess I ain't being too helpful after all. Who shall we call next?"

"No more calls. It's more than I can handle. Tell me about the fishing trip you took to the Keys."

After he left, Wynn lay back and thought about her situation. The hospital wasn't throwing her out, but someone from billing had already stopped by to tell her they'd checked her insurance and knew that she had a deductible of several thousand dollars. Now it turned out she wouldn't be able to claim on her home insurance. Which made her dependent on the cops finding the hit-and-run driver—and she had to hope like hell that he had good car insurance. She felt herself getting angry. She'd always been proud of how mild-mannered and easygoing she was, but right now if that guy was in front of her and she had use of her arms, she would have beat him to a pulp.

Wynn felt the rage inside her building. Part of it was directed inward. Why had she chosen a health plan with such a high deductible? Yes, she was healthy, but anyone could get sick or have an accident. She knew why. With the girls in college, she was always trying to find savings, and having a low premium had been part of it. But why hadn't she thought to insure her business? She'd attended all those networking meetings and listened to the insurance brokers sell their wares, yet she'd never thought it pertained to her. She'd always figured she could manage if she got the flu or some other illness that made her miss work for a couple of weeks. But this was different. This was going to be months, not weeks. She was to blame for part of her misfortune, but it was the driver of that SUV who was the cause of it all.

She wondered whether Officer Delgado was really invested in helping her. She'd heard the judgment in his tone when he found her and asked how much she'd been drinking. She'd had a sense that she was a bother to him. He might say he'd find the driver but would he, really? Maybe he was well-meaning, but to him it was just a job. She needed someone who really cared to help track down the driver. Mikki had agreed to head back to school and while Tina would do it, Wynn wasn't about to involve her daughters in this. Donte would help, but only with specific tasks. It had to be someone who cared about her, but wouldn't get overinvolved like Tina might.

The obvious person was Kat. Lately Kat had been pretty wrapped up in her new romance, but Wynn was pretty sure that if she asked, Kat would come through for her. She'd call her right now and ask her. Wynn sighed and felt the tears well up again. She couldn't even make a phone call without help. She shook her head. No more tears. She was done feeling sorry for herself. The next opportunity she got, she'd call Kat, and together they'd figure out how to get justice.

CHAPTER THIRTEEN

Officer Delgado

Officer Delgado still felt guilty at how he'd treated Wynn Larimer when he first saw her lying on the ground. He told himself it was because of what he was going through with Trish that he'd started to believe the worst about people.

Just this morning his wife had yelled at him when he suggested she try to cut down on the legally prescribed oxycodone she was taking.

"You see the news. You know how addictive it is," he said, as gently as he could.

"I am not fucking addicted!" she'd screamed, slamming down the coffee he'd just brought her so hard that it spilled on the nightstand. Trish never shouted before she was injured. Didn't swear much either. Now she'd turned into someone he hardly recognized, and even though he sympathized with her pain, he was glad to leave the house every day and get away from her. He just wished his workplace was more welcoming. He was the newest deputy in the department and, although his colleagues were friendly enough, they were still keeping him at arm's length. They'd all worked together for years and didn't hide the fact that the officer he'd replaced had been particularly well-liked.

Last week, feeling low after another bad night with Trish, he'd confided in Johnson, one of the older guys in the department, about how isolated he felt.

"We care about our citizens in this town," Johnson told him. "Do something good for someone or solve a difficult case. It will go a long way to bringing you into the fold."

Up until now all his shifts had been so routine he'd had no opportunity to shine. The case with Wynn Larimer was different though. This was going to involve real police work and he was the one who would do it. If her injuries had been life-threatening, they'd have brought in the big guns from the county, but because she was just banged up he was working the case by himself. He wished she could have given him more information, but he'd meant it when he promised to find the driver. She looked so pitiful, stranded in her hospital bed, that he wanted to do right by her. And it wouldn't hurt that by being the one to bring this hit and run driver to justice he might finally earn the acceptance he craved.

The traffic light turned red and he glanced around him, idly surveying the street. Gulfport was like two towns in one: the artsy-fartsy areas with galleries and restaurants, and the area he was in now with its cut-price supermarket, a faded Chinese takeout, and a couple of empty stores that rotated between beauty parlors and seasonal tax offices. The light changed, and he was about to drive on when he noticed the auto repair shop catty-corner to where he was stopped. On the off-chance, he decided to stop there and see if there were any vehicles that could be the one he was looking for. He swung into the parking area. Almost immediately a middle-aged, heavyset white male in baggy, grease-stained trousers walked toward him, wiping his hands on a cloth he switched from one hand to the other. The guy hadn't even waited for him to walk toward the office. Del knew what that meant. He'd seen it enough times. *Let's get law enforcement off my property before any of my customers see him and wonder what's up.*

"Wally Henderson, owner, at your service. How can I help you, Officer?" Wally extended his arm, ready to shake hands with Del. The cloth he'd just used to clean his hands looked so grimy Del would have preferred not to touch any part of him, but duty called. He grasped the man's hand firmly in his and pumped it, hard.

"Just wondering if you got any SUVs in today, needing some bodywork?"

Wally shook his head. "Nah. I'm booked pretty solid. Folks have to make an appointment if they want me to work on their cars."

Del paused. It was probably true. But what if it weren't? He glanced around the forecourt, then back at Wally. Wally frowned slightly. "You're welcome to look around. I got two SUVs here right now. That Subaru—" he gestured to a blue vehicle with a back bumper hanging loose and a massive dent in the side. "That's been here for days. Still waiting on the okay from the insurance guy. "The black GLE—" he motioned toward a large expensive looking Mercedes. "He's a regular customer. Wants me to replace the sound system with one that'll blast your eardrums even more than the current one."

"And that's it?" Del didn't want to annoy the guy, but he needed to be sure.

"Like I said, take a look around. You can see for yourself what's on the lifts." Wally started to walk away.

"If someone came to you with a vehicle you couldn't fix, where would you send them?" If the driver were local, and Del still believed that was the most likely scenario, he'd have to use one of the nearby repair shops, wouldn't he? Wally turned back around.

"I don't send people anywhere. I'm the best in the area. They're better off waiting for me."

Del smiled. He liked guys who were self-confident. "I hear you. But let's say this person was in a hurry, couldn't wait for your expertise. Where would they go?"

"There's a few shops around here. My friend Jimmy does repair work, but he mostly works on RVs and trucks. Corrigan's over on Pasadena. They're a big place; you could check them out."

"Any smaller guys, not on the main drag?"

Wally cocked his head, like a large bulldog waiting for a command from its owner. "Right around the corner there's a couple of lesbian mechanics. Look more like men than I do." Wally chuckled. Del was surprised at the disparagement. Gulfport was the most liberal place he'd ever worked. Still, this was Florida and even in the most progressive towns, you could always find some rednecks. As if to confirm his suspicions, Wally added, "there's a spic up the road there." He pointed in the opposite direction from the lesbian mechanics. "Roberto, or some such. Never had any dealings with him, though. Probably wouldn't understand a word he says." Wally guffawed loudly to himself as he walked away.

Del felt a tightness in his chest. Had Wally noticed the name

Timing Is Everything

on his name-tag and purposely said something to get his goat? Del made a point of walking through the entire garage, looking at each vehicle on the forecourt and inside on the lifts, but he saw nothing that matched what he was looking for. Time to move on to the next place. He looked at his watch. Late afternoon. It might be a good time to interview Wynn's neighbors since she'd said they didn't work. He'd do that first, then work his way through the mechanics. He'd start with the guy called Roberto. He always enjoyed having a good conversation in Spanish.

CHAPTER FOURTEEN

Officer Delgado

Officer Delgado eased his cruiser to a stop in front of the small bungalow that sat on the other side of the alley from Wynn's house. Was it only last night that he'd found Wynn lying helplessly in the woodpile? He wondered if she'd noticed that he'd treated her as if she were just another drunk lying in the alley. Hopefully not, especially given the condition she was in. He was aware that for all he knew Wynn could have drunk too much. There had been no reason to breathalyze her, but he couldn't rule out that whatever had happened had been partly because she hadn't been able to react quickly enough. He exited his vehicle.

"Hi, Officer Delgado." He looked up and saw Wynn's daughter, Tina, waving at him as she emerged from the front door, along with the two rambunctious dogs he'd met last night. The moment she called to him, the dogs began straining on their leashes, trying to tear away from her, and she almost tumbled down the steps as the dogs barreled toward him.

He patted the large dog on the head. "Hey, boys, remember me?" The smaller dog was sniffing up and down his leg. "They met me last night," Del raised his head as he explained himself to Tina.

"Do you have any leads yet?" Obviously she wasn't one for social chitchat.

"Sorry. But I only came on duty a few hours ago. The first thing I did was go to see your mom, and then I stopped by one of the local auto mechanics. Right now I want to talk to your neighbors and see if they heard anything."

"Nobody's talked with them yet? What's taking so long?" Tina looked put out. She was a stocky young woman, with short cropped hair and an athletic physique. She looked exhausted. Del knew she was only trying to protect her mom, but he didn't appreciate the implied criticism.

"This is a small town; we don't have an endless supply of police officers. You're not on an episode of *CSI*." He hoped his voice didn't sound too gruff.

"But couldn't the officer on the morning shift have come over to talk to the neighbors?"

"We were short-staffed this morning. The officer who would have been assigned to help out in this zone is on vacation. Don't worry, I'm on top of things. I'll get your guy." The dogs were whining, anxious for their walk. "You better get going, sweetheart. I'll keep you and your family posted if I have anything at all to share with you."

"Thanks." Tina's face had softened a little. "But officer, I'd rather you not call me sweetheart. Just Tina is fine."

She ran off with the dogs and Del made his way up the path to the neighbor. He didn't have to ring the bell because she'd clearly been watching out of her window and was already opening the front door when he reached it. She was an elderly woman with a wide, pleasant face, leaning heavily on a metal walker. She pushed the walker to one side slightly and sank into one of the armchairs on the porch, intimating that he should do the same.

"Tina told me what happened to dear Winnie. It's terrible, quite terrible. I'm Mrs. Johnson by the way. But everyone calls me Mrs. J." She paused for a second. "Actually, I believe they call me 'Old Mrs. J.'" Her eyes twinkled. "Would you like a cup of herbal tea?"

He shook his head. "No ma'am. Thanks for the offer, but I just wanted to ask you if you heard or saw anything last night."

"Yes and no," she said.

Del cocked his head to one side and Mrs. Johnson proceeded to answer the implied question.

"Even with my hearing aids I don't hear that well. So I have to turn the TV up pretty high. Especially since . . ." she paused. Del leaned forward, and looked directly into her eyes, encouraging her to continue. "If I tell you something, you don't have to share it with anyone, do you?"

"If it's pertinent to the case, I do." His heart quickened. What did she know?

"No, I mean, you wouldn't have to tell Winnie. If it was something I didn't want her to know."

Del shook his head, slowly. "I don't think so."

The old lady leaned back in her chair. "I've never told her this, because she's such a very dear, dear person, but, well . . . her dogs drive me bananas. They bark all the time. Every time somebody walks past the house, they bark. If someone drives down the alley, they go completely berserk. Last night was one of those nights when it seemed like they'd barely stopped barking before they started up again. Sometimes I wonder whether Winnie even hears them, or whether she's just immune to it. There are times when I turn the TV up real loud to try to drown them out. Other times, I take my hearing aids out altogether. That helps a lot. I can put the subtitles on the TV, so I can still see my favorite shows. In fact, sometimes I prefer to do that. Everyone on TV seems to talk so fast nowadays that, even with my aids in, I can't always make out what they're saying. Last night was one of those evenings when I'd taken out my aids."

Damn. Mrs. J was a talker without anything to say. Del started to stand up, but she motioned him back down.

"The thing is, I *did* think I heard something. Like a bang, or a thud. Of course almost as soon as I heard it, the dogs started up. I waited to see if I'd hear anything more, but I didn't. I know I should have gotten up to check, but when you're my age, getting up is such an effort that you don't do it unless you have to." She leaned forward and said almost conspiratorially, "I didn't even have my teeth in."

Del smiled. "I understand. My grandma still lives by herself, even though we've asked her to move in with one of us. She's sharp as a tack, but physically things take her a long time."

Mrs. J. patted his hand. "Then you understand why I didn't get up. The thing is, I'm always thinking I hear things. After I heard that first noise, I kept thinking I was hearing noises." Del figured she must have heard him pull up, and almost certainly would have heard when the ambulance arrived. "I used to get up and see what it was when I heard noises. Sometimes it was the lid blown off the trash can; other times it was people driving down the alley, foraging for used stuff that people leave out for the garbage collectors. So I've learned to keep myself busy and not dwell on the noises. I always figured if it was something serious, Winnie would come running over to tell me." As she said it, Mrs. J. shook her head from side to side as if aware of the irony. "She's such a wonderful neighbor. Sometimes she offers to go shopping for me . . . If only I had just gone out to check."

Del stood up. He had a lot to do this evening and a limited time to do it. "You didn't know," he said. "It's like the boy who cried wolf, isn't it? I appreciate what you've told me and I'll get back to you if I have any more questions."

Mrs. J's eyes filled with tears. "I do hope you catch whoever did this to our Winnie. It's not right. It's just not right."

CHAPTER FIFTEEN

Officer Delgado

The neighbor on the other side wasn't home, and Del decided now was a good time to check out the other local auto repair shops. He was convinced the driver was a local because people from other places didn't usually drive down the alleys; they stuck to the main streets. He drove over to the car repair Wally had said was owned by a man called Roberto.

It was a small shop, tucked away on a side street. Del wondered how the guy had a commercial permit in this leafy neighborhood, but he'd seen other places like this in Gulfport. It was such a pretty town, but it had some weird rules. For example, he'd quickly learned that because it was originally a fishing village, you could keep a dilapidated sailboat or a thirty-nine-foot yacht in your front yard, however much of an eyesore it was to the neighbors. But a brand-new RV half that size couldn't even be kept in your driveway, unless you were grandfathered in. Which must be how Roberto was allowed to have his shop where it was. Someone had to have been doing commercial work there for many years.

The moment he pulled in, he saw it. A large silver SUV, sitting on the forecourt with its bumper hanging down and broken headlights. He pulled the cruiser over, parked it under a towering mango tree, and then crossed the road. A sign indicating an office beckoned him through to the back. As he followed it, he realized that the place was larger than it looked. He'd thought it was just a converted bungalow with a couple of cars parked out front, but now he could see it was a double or triple lot with several vehicles parked in the back. There was no sign of any workers, and he hoped he wasn't too late to catch the owner. He was relieved to see that the door to the office was open. Inside a man about his age was running his hand through dark wavy hair as he pecked out something on a computer with one finger. The man looked up when he saw Del.

"*Buenas tardes,*" Del said, "¿*eres Roberto?*"

"I'm Rico. But is it okay with you if we switch to English?" The man had a Florida twang with not even a hint of Spanish-accented English. Del felt foolish and annoyed at himself. Wally was the type who'd think that anyone with a so-called ethnic name had just got off the boat. Rico's family probably went back generations.

"Sure. Looks like you're in the middle of something though."

"Trying to get caught up on paperwork. My least favorite part of this job."

"Tell me about it. We go into jobs for the action and there always seems to be more paperwork than anything else. You always been a car mechanic?"

"I'm more of a detailer, but yeah, I've loved cars since I was a kid. However, I'm sure you're not here to listen to my nostalgic stories. What can I do for you?"

Rico was at ease and friendly. If he knew anything about what had happened to the SUV out front, he certainly was good at covering it up.

"That bashed-in silver Hyundai I saw—know how it got like that?"

A shadow crossed Rico's face. "Why are you asking?"

"I'm looking for a hit-and-run driver. This may be the vehicle he was driving."

An expression crossed Rico's face that Del couldn't quite figure out. Concern? Anxiety? Fear? Del's antenna went up. Rico knew something, Del was sure of it.

"I doubt it. That's my cousin's car. I'm just doing her a favor, fixing it up."

"Had it here for a while?" He asked as casually as he could.

"Nah. She just brought it in, first thing this morning."

Del felt his heart race. "Did she tell you what happened?"

Rico paused again. "Said she drove into something. I don't know . . . she was in a hurry. I think you should talk to her. No point in my telling you anything she can tell you herself."

"You think she didn't want to tell you what happened?"

Rico shook his head. "No. That wasn't it. I had two customers behind her who'd both just brought in their vehicles. She didn't want to keep them waiting. And she had to get to work."

"But surely you needed the details of what happened for the insurance company?"

"She's not making a claim."

"Really?" Del's antenna felt like it had just received an electric shock. "Isn't this going to be an expensive repair job without using insurance?"

"That's why she brought it to me. She knows I'll keep it as low as possible. Sure, the insurance companies pay, but when you're the at-fault driver, they jack up the premium so much afterward you end up losing out anyway."

Rico wiped the back of his sleeve across his forehead. He was starting to sweat, despite the chill in the air. Was the conversation making him uncomfortable? Del hated that the perpetrator might be a member of his own community, and he was surprised that it was a woman, but he was becoming more and more sure he'd found the right person.

"If you'll just give me her name and address . . ." he said.

§

Fifteen minutes later, Del pulled up outside a two-story lemon-yellow stucco apartment complex. Carefully trained bougainvillea made its way up the left side of the building, its purple blossoms a riotous contrast to the recently painted turquoise trim. Each apartment had either a patio or a small balcony. You could tell a lot about the people who lived there by looking at what they kept on their balconies, and this one showed well. Potted plants, small tables with deck chairs, a couple of rainbow flags. None of the balconies were crammed full of broken appliances, bicycles with flat tires and trailing chains or abandoned strollers, like the apartments on the other side of town.

Del glanced down at his notebook for the apartment number.

Johnson had laughed the first time he saw Del pull out a stubby pencil and scribble down an address. "Why not use your phone or tablet? Nobody uses pen and paper anymore." But it made Del feel more like a real cop, the kind he'd seen on TV when he was a boy and decided that one day he too would join law enforcement. He climbed the stairs, then rapped on the door of the first apartment on the left.

"Gabriella Luna?" He asked when the door was answered by a rather stunning-looking woman with dark hair and a bosom he'd have to work hard to avoiding staring at.

She nodded and cocked her head to one side. "Can I help you?"

"My name is Officer Delgado and I'm just making some routine inquiries. May I come in?"

She stepped aside, and he followed her into a bright, airy living room. A small child in shorts and a yellow, SpongeBob T-shirt was grabbing at a building block from the pile surrounding him. Del was never any good at guessing ages, though he could see the child was more than a toddler. The mop of curls on the child's head made it difficult to assess whether it was a boy or girl, but either way he was impressed by the kid's clear enjoyment as it placed a block carefully at an angle to the one next to it. Invariably when he went into people's homes the children were staring with blank expressions at blaring TV screens, or immersed in small portable electronic devices. It had been a long time since he'd seen building blocks.

"What you makin'?" He squatted down by the kid, still unsure whether it was male or female.

"A fortress." The child looked up briefly, then went back to work.

"Please," Gordy indicated a chair at the small round dining table in one corner of the room. "Take a seat."

He liked her right away, though he wished he didn't. It always made it harder when he was talking to a suspect. She was being polite but he could see by the awkward way she stood, rubbing her right foot against the back of her left leg, that he was making her nervous. Most people got anxious when a uniformed officer showed up at their door, whether or not they were guilty of anything. Heck, he himself would slam on the brakes when he was driving his own vehicle on the freeway if he saw a highway patrol or law enforcement speed trap vehicle, even if he was well within the speed limit. He noticed she rubbed her hands on the side of her dress before she took a seat opposite him at the table. It wasn't warm, but she was sweating.

Unable to think of any small talk, he plunged right ahead. "You're the owner of a silver Hyundai Tucson?"

"Yes, but it's not here right now. It's in the shop, being repaired."

Del was relieved that she'd answered in a way that his next question would appear totally natural.

"What happened?"

"I was driving home and . . ." she paused and he waited to see what she'd say. "I was careless. I bashed into something. Knocked off the front bumper. Why did you want to know about my car?"

"What did you smash into?"

She didn't answer right away. Her eyes narrowed and her shoulders stiffened. He saw the change, noticed her demeanor move from being slightly guarded, the way most people were with cops, to being suspicious. He decided he'd better answer her question.

"A vehicle similar to yours was involved in an accident. I need to rule out local owners so I can narrow it down."

Surprisingly, her shoulders relaxed and she looked relieved. "Oh," she nodded, "an accident. I hope no one was seriously injured."

"An old lady."

An expression of concern crossed her face. "Oh dear, how terrible. And the driver didn't stop?" He shook his head and she continued. "That's awful. You read about that kind of thing happening in cities, but not a small town like ours. I hope she'll be okay."

He was relieved at the way she spoke. She sounded genuine, not like someone trying to cover up their actions. He was glad. A nice woman, a cute kid, a well-kept apartment, these were the type of folks who reminded him that most people were just getting on with living their lives, no muss, no fuss. After he spoke to Rico, he'd been hopeful that he could solve this case quickly. It was frustrating to think he'd hit a dead-end, but he was used to that in his line of work.

He smiled. "So it wasn't you then." He started to stand.

"No. I just hit a woodpile. I was driving down one of the alleys on the other side of Gulfport, not looking where I was going."

He'd stood up but hadn't moved away from the table, and now he sank back down in his chair. An alley in Gulfport? It was her, after all.

"Are you okay?" She asked. "Can I get you a bottle of water?"

He shook his head slowly. "Tell me where the alley was," he said, almost despondently.

CHAPTER SIXTEEN

Gabriella

"Do me a favor. Don't leave town for the next few days, okay?"

Officer Delgado stood and Gordy felt her chest constrict.

"Why?"

"As I said, I just need to rule people out."

"But why didn't what I told you rule me out? You said it was a hit-and-run. I told you I collided with a pile of wood."

"I know that's what you said. I'm also wondering why your cousin wasn't willing to tell me what happened. Was he trying to protect you?"

"No! He didn't know exactly what happened because I didn't tell him. I was in a hurry to get to work."

"Or maybe you were hiding something from him."

"No! Look, I don't understand . . ."

She watched the police officer. One minute it seemed like he was her friend, and the next he was out to get her. Now his face softened a little.

"It's just protocol, okay?"

She didn't trust him. He still hadn't told her where the hit-and-run had happened, or any details about it. She'd noticed that his demeanor had changed at some point in their interview, and he was definitely taking a more formal tone with her. Gordy didn't like it. He'd ruffled Sammy's hair when he first arrived, but now he

Timing Is Everything

ignored the boy as he made his way to the door.

"When will I know that I'm no longer a suspect?" She could barely bring herself to say the word. She opened the door to let the officer out. He turned toward her.

"Pretty soon, I hope."

***

After he left she called Rico.

"Is the car ready?"

"Should be done by tomorrow afternoon."

"No! I need it by the morning."

"Chica, I'd have to work on it all evening, and I promised Natalia we'd have a date tonight. I got a babysitter, restaurant reservation, everything."

She felt bad. She was familiar with how it felt to be parent of a newborn, though not what it was like to have a toddler as well. She had no doubt Natty was desperate to have a night out. "Please. It's urgent."

"Did that cop talk to you? Is that what this is about?"

"Yes." She walked into the kitchen. Sammy didn't need to hear this conversation. He'd seemed pretty oblivious when the officer was here, but you never knew with him. She'd be convinced he was blissfully unaware of a conversation and then all of a sudden he'd pipe up with something that showed he'd paid attention to every word. Like last week when she and Rico were sitting on the porch while Sammy was immersed in showing Rico Junior how to put Lego pieces together. Sammy had been chattering away demonstrating and explaining how to push the pieces into each other. After they left Rico's place Sammy had suddenly piped up with, "Why does having a baby mean they don't have sex anymore?" She'd almost fallen through the floor.

She stood by the kitchen sink and contemplated attacking the pile of dishes in it. "What exactly did you tell that cop when he asked about my car?"

"I didn't. I said if he wanted to know what happened, he should talk to you."

"He thought that was suspicious behavior. I said I hadn't had time to tell you anything."

"Which was true. But I don't understand. Why does he think you're involved? You weren't in no hit-and-run, were you, Cuz?"

"No. I told him. I was driving down an alley and drove into a pile of wood. I explained exactly what happened. Well, except for the fact that I was texting. I didn't tell him that."

"You sure it was just wood? Was it dark? Could you see?"

"I got out of the car to double-check what I hit."

"Well, then, you'll be fine. He's just being officious."

With her spare hand, Gordy pulled out a saucepan from under the sink so she could heat up mac and cheese for Sammy.

"I don't know..." She rummaged in the cupboard.

"Why did you say you need the car tomorrow morning? What's the big rush?"

Gordy couldn't open the carton of food with one hand so she stood still, saying nothing.

"Dios mío, Gordy, don't do anything foolish. You're overreacting. Nothing's going to happen to you."

"You don't know that. You know what could happen if I get arrested."

"Don't be paranoid. Nothing would happen. You're fine. You're—"

Gordy slammed the package on the kitchen counter and grabbed the phone with both hands. "You don't know! You can't be sure. You have no idea what it's like, living like this. Please. I don't know what I'm going to do, but give me the option. Just have the car ready for me first thing tomorrow morning, I beg you. Tell Natty I'll babysit every day for a week if she just lets you work late tonight."

Rico sighed heavily. "You are going to owe me so big, you have no idea."

"Thank you, cousin, thank you. Maybe I *am* being paranoid. But this way, I'll have options available to me while I think it all through."

***

By the morning, Gordy had convinced herself that Rico was right; she was overreacting. She rose early and made Sammy his favorite breakfast, waffles with chocolate chips.

"On a weekday?" His eyes were wide, but he dug his fork quickly into the waffle as if she might change her mind at any second. She smiled and packed his lunch box.

"We're walking again," she said, ignoring the grimace he made. "Maybe tomorrow I'll drive you to school, once I get the car back from Tío Rico." He looked slightly mollified.

The newest *Gulfport Gazette* weekly was in the box at the end of the street and she picked one up. While she and Sammy waited for a gap in traffic so they could cross the road, she flipped idly through the pages.

Gulfport police are looking for the person who broke into Mrs. Compton's home on Beach Blvd and stole several valuable items including the silver mermaid sculpture her late husband commissioned for their diamond anniversary. Gulfportians know Mrs. Compton as the ever-present matriarch who invited the entire community to stop by her home and help her celebrate her ninety-eighth birthday last year. Anyone with any information about the robbery should contact Officer Blackburn at ext. 3634.

What a shame, Gordy thought. She remembered the event they were referring to. There had been a crowd in front of the house as she and Sammy walked by, and the old lady, who was barely taller than the purple hibiscus bush in her front yard, had reached her hand out to Sammy and asked him to shake it. Sammy had looked at the bony knuckles and paper-thin skin, touched the brown marks on her hand, and then asked her whether she had the measles. She'd smiled and told him that if he were lucky enough to reach the age she had, likely he too would get liver spots.

"Mom!" Sammy had been tugging on her sleeve and now she'd missed the pedestrian light.

"Sorry, sweetie," she said, "it'll change again soon."

She looked down at the next item.

Gulfport police are investigating a hit-and-run that occurred in the alley between 24th and 25th Avenue off Ohio Street on Tuesday night. An elderly woman was knocked to the ground and left there. She was transported to the hospital with serious injuries. The vehicle, believed to be a white or silver-gray newer model SUV, fled the scene. Anyone with any information should contact Officer Delgado at ext. 3636.

The blood rushed to her head and she felt shaky all over. For a moment she was so dizzy she thought she would faint. An alley. It had happened in an alley. When Officer Delgado interviewed her, he'd implied it was something that happened in the street. Or maybe she'd assumed that. No wonder his attitude toward her had changed when she mentioned she was driving up an alley. She wasn't sure if the one mentioned in the article was the same alley she'd driven down, but she did know it had been off Ohio in just that area. She scanned the item again. It didn't say what time the hit-and-run had occurred—perhaps they didn't know—but everything matched: Tuesday night, that location, the vehicle color and model.

But she checked! She'd gone back to see what she'd hit, and she would definitely have seen or heard if someone had been lying there. Wouldn't she?

"What's the matter, Mami?" Sammy had put his hand in hers, ready to cross the road. The traffic had cleared and he was waiting, looking up at her expectantly.

"I—nothing."

Was it her? What if she'd shone her flashlight in the wrong direction and seen only the woodpile and not a woman who'd been knocked over. But it couldn't be. She'd have heard her moaning. It must have been someone else who drove down there after she did. But what if there were no one else? Or what if the police didn't care whether there was someone else because they'd already fingered her for it? She stood for a moment longer. She couldn't risk it. Couldn't risk being arrested, whether it was her or not. "Sammy, I just remembered, you don't have to go to school today. Come with me to Tio Rico to get the car."

"But, Mami, we do have school today. See, there's Jamal and Kenisha crossing the road over there. And I promised Devon I'd give him my sandwich from my lunch box. Oh, I mean . . ."

Sammy clapped his hand across his mouth, but Gordy had no time to think about what he was saying. Her mind was a jumble, but one thought was emerging from the chaos. She had to get away. As she dragged Sammy away from the school, she started making a plan. First she had to call in sick at work. Then she had to go shopping. Lastly, she had to fill the car's tank with gas. As much as it would take.

CHAPTER SEVENTEEN

May, Two Years Earlier

Gabriella

It was the day they'd all been excited about and dreading at the same time. The day they'd find out the future of their research project. Gordy was desperately trying to focus on completing data entry, but, like everyone else in the department, she was having difficulty concentrating.

"What time do you think we'll know?" she asked her supervisor, Dr. Chin, as he walked by her desk.

"They said we'd hear some time today. On other grants they've let us know first thing in the morning. I'm sure we'll be safe. We have really good data and our study is important. Longitudinal studies on the elderly are more vital than ever with our graying boomer population."

"I know. But it's not a sexy topic, is it?"

"Don't be so cynical, Gabriella. It's not like you. These funders aren't about sexy."

"I still don't see why we had to reapply for the funding. We're ten years in. Surely they wouldn't abandon a study after all that time?"

Gordy sat back in her chair. There was no point even attempting to enter the data, and she noticed Dr. Chin didn't seem to be able to focus on his work either. He'd been pacing back and forth through their suite all morning, gripping his phone tightly in his fist. He stood facing her, his butt leaning against a table opposite Gordy's desk.

"I hate to ask you this, but what will you do if it doesn't come through?" His expression was sympathetic. He knew that she depended on this job for her visa and had been supportive of her from the first day she started working for him.

"I'm not even going there. I'm determined to stay positive. Once the funding is secure for the next five years, I really think I'll be in with a good shot getting my green card. I've been looking into it, and I think I could get a National Interest Waiver."

"I thought you said you couldn't get a green card based on your work because you have to prove nobody else is currently qualified to do it and you can't prove that."

"I know. A National Interest Waiver is usually given to foreign celebrity sports players and the like, but I heard about a social worker who got her card that way. She was compiling a manual for attorneys defending battered women accused of murdering their abusers, and they said that work was in the national interest. Our work is important to this country too."

"I hope you're right."

Gordy hoped so too. She'd never expected this path toward citizenship to take so long. She'd been enamored of the USA ever since her parents had brought her to New York for a family wedding when she was twelve years old. Her cousin had married a mathematics professor who taught at Columbia, and the ceremony was in the awe-inspiring St. Paul's Chapel on the grounds of the university. A seed had been planted in Gordy's brain, that one day she would apply to Columbia. There was something thrilling about New York, and she'd felt a level of excitement in everything she did there: walking through the famed Central Park and admiring the skyscrapers all around, shopping on renowned Fifth Avenue, lining up for half-price theater tickets at Times Square. Guadalajara was beautiful, but it couldn't match the buzz of Manhattan. She'd made a vow that she would try to spend at least a year in the USA at some point in her life. She'd stopped speaking Spanish at home and annoyed her friends by demanding they only speak English to her so that by the time she arrived in America her accent was almost undetectable.

Ten years ago she started applying to master's degree psychology programs in the USA and discovered that getting accepted was harder than she expected. She settled for a place at Florida University even though it wasn't Columbia, and Hillsborough County definitely wasn't Manhattan. But the tropical summer weather reminded her of home and the nearby coast was beautiful. When she'd first received her student visa to come to the USA, she assumed she'd stay two years to do her master's, possibly get one year of experience, and then go back home. But at the end of two years, the university had encouraged her to apply for her doctorate and had helped her with the new visa application process. Two years into the degree, they offered her a job as a research assistant and she switched to an H1B visa, which gave her three more years. The research dovetailed perfectly with her dissertation, and she was all set to finish up her doctorate and become a professor. But then life happened.

First, she was promoted to program manager which meant that in addition to collecting and analyzing all the research data, she was also in charge of program administration. That left her with a lot less time and inclination to pursue her studies. Then she discovered gay night life in Tampa. She'd been so focused on her studies that for years she'd had no time for socializing. But when she discovered La Morena nightclub she also found out that late-night dancing was a lot more fun than hours buried in the dry, academic material she needed to wade through to write up a dissertation. She worked hard, played hard, and when she met Dana, she shoved her dissertation research in the bottom of a filing cabinet and enjoyed the dizzy sensation of falling in love. When the H1B expired, she was able to get it renewed for another three years to continue her position as program manager. By then she and Dana were living together and she was three months pregnant. She still had no permanent way to stay in the USA, which made her anxious, but she mostly didn't think about the future too much.

Gordy's dissertation chair had stopped asking her when she was going to have something for him to look at, but her mamá hadn't.

"Please, hija, cover your bases," her mother begged on the phone. "What if the job falls through? You'll have nothing. They'll kick you out of the country."

"The job won't fall through. It's an amazing program, helping drug-addicted elderly clients. My position is key—services are important, but collecting data on service utilization, recidivism rates, and all the other stuff is essential. I'll find a way to stay here, don't worry."

Her mother would put her father onto the phone to try his luck.

"If I can't get a green card any other way, I'll just have to get married," she joked with her father when he echoed her mother's concerns.

"I wish you would," he said gruffly, "and I don't mean to that 'friend' you live with now. I wish you'd let your cousin Rico introduce you to a nice young man."

"Papa, how many times do I have to tell you she's not my friend; she's my partner. We have a child together. I was just joking about getting married."

It was so frustrating. Any straight person in her position would have been married by now with a legal green card and without all the stress and uncertainty that being a noncitizen entailed.

"You're an alien!" Her sister would scoff. "Why would you want to live somewhere that treats you as if you're from outer space?"

She couldn't explain it to Amalia, but she loved America and she loved Florida. Despite the government calling her an alien, everyone she knew treated her well. Americans assumed she'd left Mexico because it was hard being gay, and she had to explain to them that it was pretty similar in both countries: in any large city there was plenty of gay acceptance and Mexico was no different. She'd attended Guadalajara's Pride event for years before she came to the States. There were things about her hometown that she missed, like wandering through the cobbled streets of the old city, but she hated the traffic snarls and pollution, and she disliked the snobbism too. Americans had no idea that her own family looked down on the working class Mexicans and paesanos even more than they did. No, America was her future and she was determined to stay here.

Dr. Chin's phone buzzed, and he looked down quickly at the text message coming in. He gripped the side of the desk, and Gordy could see right away that it wasn't good news.

"Tell me," she whispered.

He read aloud, scrolling down as he did so. "Dear Grantee, after much deliberation the Committee has decided not to renew funding for your program. The committee received several proposals for this program, all of which were more competitive. The one we chose, Pathways to Prosperity, has promised to continue the longitudinal studies of the addicted geriatric population that made your program unique. We wish Florida University well in your future endeavors and encourage you to apply for future funding cycles for other programs. As you know, the current cycle ends in six months. As a reminder, your original contract, along with the renewal contract signed five years ago, requires that you fully cooperate with the new organization to ensure a smooth transition of clients and data."

Gordy was stunned. She'd convinced herself that the program was secure. But there was a glimmer of hope. "Pathways to Prosperity isn't academic. Do you think they'll want to keep us on so we can ensure the research for the study is done properly?"

Dr. Chin shook his head slowly. "They'll probably hire some of our program staff and maybe the research assistant. But PTP will bring in their own project manager and project director. And I don't believe for a moment they'll really keep the study going. Not at the level we did. They'll do basic data collection, enough to keep the county and state happy, but the real information will be lost. No, my dear, I'm afraid this is the end of the road for you and me."

§

"What will I do?" Gordy groaned over and again as she stood at the bottom of the wavy slide in the local park, watching Dana coax Sammy to be brave and push off on his own.

"Mami too!" He squealed. Gordy gave in and climbed the steps of the slide, then sat at the top, her legs spread so Sammy could sit between them, her arm tight around his waist. She pushed off and as she slid to the bottom, she couldn't help feeling the downward spiral was a metaphor for her life.

"You'll apply for another job," said Dana as she scooped Sammy up.

"I keep telling you, it's not that simple. They're not going to approve another H1B. It was one thing when the university sponsored me, but nobody's going to hire someone who most likely won't be approved."

"What about that other visa you mentioned, the one where

you prove your work is in the national interest? Why can't you go for that?"

Gordy shook her head in frustration. Dana didn't get it. She had no idea what it was like to live in limbo and have absolutely no sense of security. The house was in Dana's name, the car was in Dana's name, everything had to be done through Dana. Thank goodness Sammy would always be a citizen and would never know what it was like to be treated this way.

"¡Ven a casa! Come home," said Mamà when she told her parents what had happened.

"You always have a home here. You and the little one," said her father. Gordy didn't know whether he had purposely excluded Dana or not.

Dana didn't speak Spanish and had no desire to leave the US. The only time they'd gone to Guadalajara together, it had seemed to Gordy that Dana had blinders on. She'd convinced herself that Mexico was a backward country and couldn't see the charm and beauty of it. Gordy took her into the historic center, with its plazas and churches, and to the humongous outdoor market. The only thing Dana commented on were the huge rumps of pigs hanging from hooks.

"They stink," she said, holding her nose as she walked through the stalls, oblivious to the fragrant aromas of spices and herbs, and paying no attention to the juicy papayas and exotic vegetables.

"Why do they take so long to serve you?" she asked impatiently, unable to relax in the slow-paced ambiance of the restaurant in Zapopan that Gordy and her family loved so much.

"They're so loud and out of key," she complained when the mariachi band serenaded them at the outdoor cafe in Tlaquepaque, after they'd shopped the delightful stores filled with blown glass, ornamental ceramics, leather goods, and brightly colored paintings.

That was before Sammy was born, and Gordy hadn't been back home since. She still thought of it as home, but home was also Florida with its grouper sandwiches and key lime pie, stately palm trees and the azure waters of the Gulf.

Now all that was in jeopardy. Her visa would expire with her job and if she stayed after the project was over, she'd be illegal.

"Let's find her a nice gay guy to marry," said Dana's friend Charlene later that evening as the three of them sipped on pinot noir during women's night at the local gay bar. "What about Peter?"

"The guy who does drag shows on the weekends?" Dana laughed. "Yeah right. You do know immigration checks up on people, don't you? Peter marrying a woman would scream fake marriage. Then for sure Gordy would be out on her ear."

Gordy hated that Dana and Charlene joked about her status. There was nothing funny about it.

Friday, June 26, 2015

It was ten o'clock in the morning, and they were sitting on the sofa next to each other, barely daring to watch TV. A month earlier she'd thought her whole future depended on the renewal of a grant. Now it depended on the Supreme Court. When everyone knew that was the day the announcement would be made, she'd called in to say she was staying home so she and Dana could watch together.

"Don't worry about it. Nobody here will be doing much work," said Dr. Chin. "We're keeping our fingers crossed for you."

Gordy had been aware that the Supreme Court was due to rule, but nobody really expected the decision to be in their favor. At work, she'd been certain the Commission would extend their funding, but at home she'd never been convinced they'd win the right to same-sex marriage. Yet the longer the decision was delayed, the more the press seemed to think they were in with a chance.

And then suddenly they heard the stunning words that seemed almost impossible.

"In a landmark decision, the Supreme Court has just ruled that gay Americans have the right to marry in all 50 states . . ." The reporter was still talking, but the cheer that had gone up in the crowd drowned out what he was saying and Dana and Gordy found themselves sobbing in each other's arms.

It was incredible, unbelievable, astounding. The TV newscaster sounded happy and the people surrounding him were delirious.

"Aren't you proud?" Dana said, pulling away from the embrace and wiping her eyes. "Now you can be an American and know that this is what our democracy is all about."

It wasn't the time to point out that same-sex marriage had been legal in Mexico City for years. No, now was the time, as Dana said, to rejoice in her adopted country's incredible ruling. She and Dana were free to marry! Which meant she could apply for a temporary green card. And that would give her the right to stay in the country and get whatever job she damn well pleased.

Marrying someone she wasn't sure she was still in love with was a small price to pay for all of that.

July 2015

They wore their best clothes and came to the immigration office loaded with photo albums and every conceivable document they could think of. The new building was beautiful, but inside it wasn't so different from the old one: a long line just to get into the waiting room, and children running around everywhere.

Gordy and Dana took their seats, Gordy tapping her foot anxiously.

"What are you here for?" Dana asked the man seated next to her. He was an older Caucasian dressed in baggy jeans. His belly protruded from the Tampa Bay Rays T-shirt that attempted to cover it. Next to him sat a gorgeous-looking Asian woman who looked to be twenty years younger than him.

"We're applying for a green card for my spouse." He slapped the young woman on the leg playfully, but she looked annoyed.

"Me too," said Dana.

"Where is he? Doesn't he have to be here too?"

"She is." Dana intimated Gordy. The man looked from one to the other, and Gordy waited for some caustic remark to follow.

"Wow. You did that gay marriage thing? Cool."

"Actually," Gordy leaned over, "it's not gay marriage. It's just marriage."

Dana frowned, but Gordy was so anxious she couldn't really make small talk.

"Don't worry," said the woman on the other side of her, a middle-aged white woman. "When I came for my appointment, the whole thing only took five minutes. The interviewer asked us how

Timing Is Everything

we met. We told him it was through an online dating service. He asked to see our marriage and drivers' licenses, checked we'd filled out all the documents, and then said everything looked fine. Now we're here for the naturalization."

The woman looked over at her husband, who squeezed her hand. "I can't believe this whole thing is finally over," she said. "Although to tell you the truth, until I have that certificate in my hand, I'm not counting my chickens." She had a strong brogue and Gordy couldn't tell what it was. Irish? Australian?

The couple on their left were called in to their appointment. Sure enough, they came out within ten minutes. The man pulled his T-shirt over his stomach. "Told you," he said. "Nothing to it." His wife was already over by the door. Gordy wondered if that marriage would last longer than the two years required for the woman to get her permanent green card. The couple on the other side of them were called, and still they sat.

"Why's it taking so long?" Gordy asked, though she knew Dana would have no idea. Her mouth was dry, and she went over to the restroom so she could gulp some water from the water fountain outside of it.

An hour and a half went by. "Look." Dana nudged Gordy and pointed to two men coming out from the interview area, holding hands and smiling at each other. "Maybe they just got married too!"

"Number 95," the loudspeaker announced.

"That's us," Dana said and Gordy felt herself tremble. She reminded herself that it was just a formality, that everyone had been coming and going pretty quickly. She gripped their photo albums with both arms across her chest.

"I'm very sorry to keeping you waiting," the agent said with a heavy Russian accent. She was middle-aged, a large cross dangling over the buttons of a uniform that was straining against her chest. "Last couple, very difficult case." Gordy wondered, as she always did when she was at the immigration center, why so many of the staff were non-native speakers. She supposed it was so that they could work with those immigrants who didn't speak much English. "You here for . . . ?"

"Conditional Permanent Residence for Gabriella Luna," Dana said quickly, "based on immediate relative of U.S. citizen."

The agent looked up from one to the other. "And you are . . .

her sister?"

Dana smiled. "No. I'm her wife. We just got married. Now we're here for Gabriella to get her temporary green card."

The woman looked again from Gordy to Dana and back. Then she leaned back in her chair.

"Ah yes. Now we get all these new applications. People like you. Why you think we believe this marriage is real?"

"It's the law! The Supreme Court said—" Gordy burst out but the agent waved her hand in the air as if swatting Gordy away like a fly.

"No. I mean, why you think *I* believe that *this* marriage is real?"

Gordy felt herself crumpling inside. So much for an easy interview, a quick five minutes. They'd obviously got the one person who had decided it was her job to make life difficult for everyone else. Now she knew why the previous clients had been "difficult." It must have been the two men they'd seen exiting a few minutes earlier. *But they were smiling*, she told herself; *however hard she made it for them, those guys were smiling.*

"Show me documents."

They pushed the file across the table, and she picked them up and tapped on her computer as she verified each one.

"Show me wedding pictures."

Gordy opened the album. They'd gone back and forth on whether to buy the kind of embossed album some couples had with expensive pictures mounted carefully, one per page, but in the end, they'd decided they wanted to have a more natural-looking album. The agent flipped through the book, going back and forth a couple of times.

She looked up at them, a sneer on her face. "No parents. Why no parents?"

"My parents live in Mexico," Gordy said, about to explain that her father couldn't leave his business at such short notice.

"Ah. Can't get visa. I understand. No doubt, you get citizenship, your parents coming next."

Gordy was so tired of everyone assuming that all Mexicans were clamoring to get into the U.S. "They've been here plenty of times," she muttered, between gritted teeth, "They're happy in Mexico."

The agent turned to Dana. "And yours?"

"They . . . they didn't want to come. They don't accept Gabriella as my partner."

"Because she's Mexican or because she's woman?"

Gordy could see Dana was starting to get annoyed. It was the first time she'd ever had to face an immigration agent. All the times Gordy had tried to explain how frustrating and humiliating these visits and applications were, now Dana was finally seeing it for herself.

"Look. We've been together for five years," Dana said, leaning forward, her gaze steady on the officer. "We have a three-year-old son. If we could have gotten married three years ago, we would have. We've been waiting a long time to be treated just like every other citizen in this country. We've shown you far more proof of our relationship than I bet a lot of the other couples you interview have. You've seen pictures of us together in Mexico and in France. You've seen pictures of us with our son from newborn to toddler. You know perfectly well we've been a couple for years. You may not like the fact that we're married, but we are, and it's your job to give it the stamp of approval."

The agent blinked. Gordy wondered whether anyone ever stood up to her, and would have bet her next paycheck that if they did it was the American-born spouse. Gordy's stomach was completely knotted up and her throat was dry.

The agent picked up a piece of paper and handed it to them.

"It's in order. No problem." She smiled a half-smile. "But understand this." She turned to Gordy. "You do anything to discredit your marriage, we find out. You don't live together? We check. You pay her money to stay married to you? We find out." She stood up. "And don't forget, most important. You not citizen yet. You commit crime? You deported. You better be on very best behavior. Understand?"

CHAPTER EIGHTEEN

February 3

Kat

Kat was still reeling from her visit with Wynn the previous day. Poor Wynn. She'd worked so hard to build up her business, and now she was terrified it would all be lost. Not if Kat could help it. She had copied down the details from the business card the police officer had left for Wynn, and she intended to stay in close contact with him. Did he understand how much was at stake for her friend? She wasn't just injured; her entire business was at stake.

Her shift didn't start until ten so she decided to swing by the police station on the off-chance that Officer Delgado would be there. The police headquarters were housed inside City Hall so on her way to his office she stopped at the reception desk where her friend Carrie-Ann processed data for the city. Carrie-Ann also waitressed weekend shifts at The Garrett. Almost everyone in Gulfport seemed to have two jobs. Even the mayor doubled as a bartender.

"What brings you here?" Carrie Ann asked. "Unpaid traffic ticket? Or are you dropping off some of your divine lemon bars?"

"I'm stopping by to see Officer Delgado. What do you know about him?"

"Not much. He's pretty new, still finding his feet. But he's not here now. He works the late shift, 4 p.m. to 4 a.m."

"Yikes. Who'd want to work those hours?"

"He would, I guess. Gives him most of the day to take care of his personal business, though I've noticed he tends to work a lot of overtime. Sometimes he's still in the office doing paperwork when I get here at eight. And I've seen him come in as early as eleven in the morning."

The phone rang and Carrie Ann picked it up, then held the phone out at arm's length because the caller was yelling so loudly the whole office could hear her.

"Every month. Every month!" The caller yelled. "When's it going to stop?"

"Ma'am?" Carrie Ann rolled her eyes, and Kat laughed. Why were complainers always so loud? It was the same in the restaurant. People who loved her meals quietly thanked her. Those who'd found an undercooked eggplant yelled as if the entire town of Gulfport should know about it.

"It makes no sense!" The caller screamed. "Why does the city mail out a bill when I have it automatically deducted from my account?"

"We have to, Ma'am. In case you closed your bank account or—"

"I've been with the same bank for twenty years! How much money do you people waste on stamps sending bills by mail to people like me?" Carrie-Ann tried to answer, but the question was clearly rhetorical as the caller plowed right on. "We're a small town. Let's put that money to good use. Increase the library budget, or the senior center." Ah, a constructive complainer, Kat thought. Gulfport's full of those.

"It's a great idea, but I have no power over the city billing practices. Why don't you go to one of the city council meetings and—"

"Maybe I will. But will you please write down my complaint and forward it?"

Carrie Ann assured the caller she would, and hung up. "I can't tell you how many people call to ask why we waste money mailing out bills instead of emailing them. I may go to the city council meeting myself, just to get the answer."

Kat laughed. "Good to know someone cares about city finances."

"So why do you want to see Officer Del?"

"Friend of mine was a victim of a hit-and-run. He's the investigating officer."

Carrie Ann rummaged through some papers in front of her, then found what she was looking for. "This one?" She asked, holding out a copy of the local weekly. "The story I read in the *Gazette* this morning. You know her?"

Kat nodded. "Some bastard ran her down and then just left her there. She's so banged up. Her arms, hips, ribs, internal injuries . . . I want to make sure they find the driver and he pays for it."

"Or she."

"Or she what?"

"He or she. How do you know the driver was a man?"

"As if a woman would ever just drive away from something like that."

Carrie Ann sighed. "You're such an idealist. Women aren't perfect you know. Sometimes they commit crimes too. Don't you watch *48 Hours*?"

Kat felt her stomach lurch. She didn't need to watch TV to know that the most unexpected of women could end up having a dark side. Carrie-Ann was a new enough friend not to know what had happened last year. Like that cop. Which reminded her, she was wasting time. Officer Delgado wasn't there and she needed to get to work.

"Take care, Carrie Ann. Keep 'em honest."

§

Kat was sprinkling parsley into the tabbouleh she'd just cooked when the swinging door to the kitchen burst open. Kat was about to tell whoever had flung themselves through it that customers weren't allowed back there, when she looked up and saw that it was the person she most wanted to see in the whole world.

"Gordy!" She rushed to the sink to wash the parsley garnish off her fingertips. "You're not at work?"

"No time for explanations." Gordy reached into her purse, pulled something out, and thrust it toward Kat. "I need you to take this."

It was a slip of paper with a phone number scrawled on it. Kat took a step back. "What's going on?"

"The cops think I committed a crime."

"You—"

"I didn't."

"Of course you didn't. Did someone accuse you of something? Is it work-related?"

"No. An officer came to my house last night and interviewed me. Look I'll tell you the whole thing when I call you."

"What's this phone number?" Kat asked, holding out the slip of paper.

"My new number for now. I got a burner phone. I don't want anyone to be able to trace my calls."

"I don't understand." Kat put the paper down on the counter and wiped her hands on her apron. "What's going on?"

"I don't have time to explain anything right now. I'm going out of town for a few days."

"The police think you committed a crime and you're fleeing? But that makes it look as if you're guilty. Why would you leave town if you're not?"

Gordy's face had taken on a stubborn look, but beneath it Kat could see fear. What was she so afraid of? "I'm not guilty."

"Then why run? Why not stay and face the music? I'll be here. You must have other friends. We can support you, deal with whatever happens."

"No! I can't risk being arrested."

"Look, I don't know anything about the law. But I do know that if you're in trouble, the last thing you should do is skip town."

"Do you trust me, Katya?" Kat felt Gordy's gaze scorching into her, and she was like a soft piece of butter melting beneath it.

"Yes, but the police in this town are good guys. They're not going to make any kind of false arrests. Stay here and see it through."

Gordy shook her head. Tears were forming in the corners of her eyes. "You of all people should understand," she said softly. Kat didn't know what she meant. She cocked her head to one side. Gordy grabbed her arm and pulled her over to the pantry, out of earshot of anyone else who might enter the kitchen.

"I'm not a citizen." Gordy whispered.

"I know. So what?"

"Until I get my citizenship, if I commit a crime I can still be deported."

"But you just said you didn't commit one."

"It doesn't matter. If they arrest me for a felony offense, ICE can start deportation proceedings."

"Even before the trial? I don't believe it!"

Gordy shook her head impatiently. "Of course you don't. Citizens never understand the fears of noncitizens. But I thought perhaps you would."

Kat had a sudden memory of one of her mother's friends, Margalit, crying in their kitchen. Kat thought it was because Margalit was grieving the sudden death of her husband, Itai, from a heart attack. The family had come to the US because Itai was a subcontractor for the government. Margalit's daughter, Avital, was a junior at Kat's high school and everyone was being super nice to her.

"It's not bad enough, I lost my husband, now they're telling me I have to leave!" Margalit had wailed. Kat had been sitting in the corner of the room and was shocked to hear what Margalit was saying. Her mother had hugged her friend tightly as the tears streamed down Margalit's face.

"*Ma pitom*?" She shook her head in confusion. "Why should you leave?"

"Because Itai was here on a work visa. Now he's gone, Avital and I have no legal standing." After Margalit left, Kat remembered asking *Ima* what would happen.

"I don't know Kit-Kat. Margalit ought to fight it. But without Itai's salary she can't afford a lawyer."

"But if they were here at the invitation of the US government and they've lived here for all these years, why wouldn't they just let them stay?" Her mother told her it was more complicated than that. It was all about different types of visas, not about individuals.

"Can Avital stay with us so she can finish high school? Surely they'll let her do that."

Her mother shook her head. "Avital has no more right to be here than her *ima*. They'll both have to leave." And indeed, within two months Margalit and Avital were back in Tel Aviv.

Kat and her mom had felt terrible. Margalit and Avital had lost their entire support system at a time when they'd most needed one. Kat's mom found an immigration lawyer who said that he would take the case pro bono, but that it would take months or even years to resolve. Margalit said it would be too late; by then her daughter would be drafted into the army, so she turned down the chance to appeal.

Kat remembered how unfair the whole thing had been, but she understood a little bit more about visas these days. Itai had been here on a working visa. Gordy had a green card and was almost a citizen. Surely that meant something. How could Gordy be deported before she'd been found guilty?

"Don't run. Please. It can only make matters worse."

Gordy's usually strong frame looked like a tent after the stakes had been pulled, sagging and falling within itself.

"I don't know what to do." Her voice was quiet, defeated. "I don't want to flee, but I can't risk being at my apartment or going to work in case they come to arrest me. I spent last night reading everything I could on the internet, and all the stories were awful. People post questions to immigration lawyers, and the attorneys answer that they can't guarantee anything. They're seeing all kinds of egregious stuff, including things that happen to people before their cases are resolved in court. Even in situations where you'd think the person had a really strong case. And this isn't just about me. Can you imagine what it would be like for Sammy if I got deported?"

Kat had seen images on TV of immigrant parents being dragged away from their children. She still hadn't met Sammy, but she couldn't imagine what it would be like for mother or child to be separated with no idea when they'd see each other again. She understood why Gordy wanted to avoid arrest, but she couldn't let her leave.

"Stay at my house," she said. "Bring Sammy with you and stay with me for a while. The cops won't know where you are and I won't tell anyone. When I come home tonight, you'll tell me exactly what's going on and what they're accusing you of."

Gordy's eyes had an expression in them like a glimmer of sunshine peeking out after a heavy storm.

"You'll hide me?"

"It's got to be better than getting involved with burner phones." She grinned, and Gordy looked sheepish.

Gordy wavered. "It wasn't the way I was planning on introducing you to Sammy," she said. "Are you sure?"

Kat grabbed Gordy's hands. "Yes. Go home and get what you need. And bring some toys—the only ones I have are for cats."

"Oh." Gordy recoiled.

"What?"

"Sammy's allergic."

"How bad? I keep my place pretty well-vacuumed, and I can keep the cat in my room." Kat put her hand on Gordy's chin and tipped it up. "As long as he can breathe, it's better than you skipping town."

Gordy nodded slowly. Kat dug into her pocket, pulled out her key ring and slid her house key off it. She took Gordy's hand, put the key in her palm, and closed her girlfriend's fingers around it.

"It was gonna happen sooner or later anyway." She pulled Gordy toward her and felt a surge of strength. "We're going to kick this thing. I know you don't have a criminal bone in your body."

After Gordy left, Kat felt as if she were standing a little taller, her frame larger, taking up more space in the room. She felt powerful. It was an entirely new feeling to be the strong one. Kat was used to being a follower, not a leader, and it felt odd to be in the position of protecting her lover. It definitely wasn't a role she was used to. Part of what attracted her to potential mates was their aura of power. When Gordy had walked into the Dolphin Dive, Kat had been attracted not only to her external looks but to an inner strength she exuded. Right now, though, that strength was gone. Gordy was like a balloon that had soared into the air, had become entangled in tree branches, and was now a crumpled mess. Kat felt glad she could be the one to rescue her. After all, wasn't love all about being strong for the other person when they needed you?

The funny thing was that it was the second time in one day that she'd taken on this role. This morning she had gone looking for Officer Delgado, determined to help Wynn. And she was still just as determined to get justice for her friend. Now she was going to protect the woman she loved as well. Ironic that after a year when she'd reveled in the fact that nothing untoward had happened, all of a sudden both her lover and her best friend were in trouble and she was the one who could help them both. It was a great feeling.

CHAPTER NINETEEN

Officer Delgado

It was only 11.00 a.m., but Del was already sitting in his patrol car, drinking coffee and reviewing his case. His shift didn't start until noon, but he had plenty of reasons to come in early: improve his standing in the unit, help a victim in need, and get away from his wife. And if he were honest, getting away from Trish was probably reason number one.

He stared at a couple enjoying their lattes at one of the wrought iron tables on the patio. They were holding hands across the table, smiling and talking animatedly. He could remember when that's how he and Trish used to be. Now she stayed home in a darkened living room, her feet on the sofa, her back propped up with cushions so she could sit up and play video games all day. She did nothing, and if he tried to encourage her to try anything, she ignored him or complained that he didn't understand her. If only she hadn't had that fall at work. And if only that damn doctor hadn't been so willing to prescribe oxy to relieve her pain. Everyone except Trish could see she'd turned into a zombie, and an unpleasant one at that. But she refused to hear it.

"I'm in pain!" She'd yell whenever he or one of her few remaining friends tried to suggest she cut back. "None of you know how I feel."

It was true. He didn't know how it felt to be in constant physical pain, but he had a strong sense of what constant emotional pain felt like. He lived it every day. At the beginning he'd been the most supportive husband anyone could be. He'd cooked, cleaned, done all the housework, and taken Trish to the myriad appointments that ensued. He validated her when she tried shiatsu massage, acupuncture, and chiropractic. When none of those worked, he went with her to a spinal doctor who promised surgery would cure her. Despite his misgivings, he supported her decision to undergo the surgery and when she was pain-free for two weeks, he thought it had all been worthwhile. Then one day she said the pain was back, just as bad as before. She found a new doctor who said he couldn't suggest any treatment other than pain management and started her on heavy doses of Fentanyl and Dilaudid.

That had been three months ago. She was still on disability, although that wouldn't last for much longer. Which was the reason he needed to take courses and raise his salary. If they were going to keep the condo, they'd need a better income than his current one. He was a little sorry now that he'd transferred to Gulfport. In the city, he'd have had more opportunities for growth. But his buddy Mack, from the police academy, had made it sound like a good idea when he got in touch with Del to tell him he was relocating and would recommend Del for his position if he wanted it.

"It's a different world than a big city like Tampa. Folks smile and wave when they see you. They bring their dogs over so you can pat them. When they stop to talk to you, it's to ask advice or offer you a cold drink. And another thing—everyone has their zone and they work it by themselves. You're not stuck with some partner you can't stand, or you have to cover for."

That was something that appealed to Del. His partner at the time, RD, was a woman determined to prove she was more macho than him, which she probably was. Spent her day cussing and yelling, and enjoyed roughing people up for no good reason. She never crossed a line whereby he could report her, but she made life unpleasant—for perps, victims, and himself. The other thing that appealed to him was how Mack described this little place he'd never heard of prior to taking the job.

"In Tampa everyone has their prescribed role, right? But in a small place like Gulfport you'll do a bit of everything. Say, for example, there's a burglary. You'll call in forensics, but you'll do the investigation yourself. Or a hit-and-run where you need to track down the driver. If the victim's injuries are life-threatening, you'll pull in the big guns from the county to take on the investigation. But if not, you can end up doing almost the entire investigation by yourself. If you hit a dead end, you can contact the detectives for advice, but if you solve it on your own, you're a hero."

He wanted badly to be that hero. Mack had assured him the team was really tight-knit, and it was true. Only he wasn't part of the knit yet. The guys said that if Mack thought Del was the right replacement for him, he was welcome on the team. To his face they were perfectly friendly. They answered his questions and showed him the ropes. But he noticed how they clammed up sometimes when he approached his desk, as if they'd been discussing something they weren't yet ready to share with him. A couple of times he'd caught them discussing a social event they'd all attended but to which they'd "forgotten" to invite him. He was hoping that solving this hit-and-run would win their approval.

Which was why he was sitting in his squad car, figuring out how to wrap up the case as quickly as possible. He reran his steps. He'd talked to that elderly neighbor who'd confirmed hearing something like a thud. But she'd never gone to see what it was, and she admitted she heard noises all the time and could have heard other noises that same night. She couldn't even distinguish between the accident and when he or the ambulance arrived. The other neighbor had been on a fishing trip, and he hadn't found any neighbors who could confirm anything for him. But when he'd gone to the auto repair shops, he'd found Gordy's vehicle right away. He'd thought it was too good to be true. Most hit-and-run drivers tried to hide their vehicles, but she'd taken hers right here in town. It had made no sense until he interviewed her and discovered she seemed genuinely unaware that she'd hit anyone.

He didn't like the idea that this friendly (and he had to admit, beautiful) woman with the cute kid was the perp. But clearly she was. She admitted driving into the woodpile where he'd found Wynn. He didn't need to overthink it. She was his guy. But right now, apart from her description of hitting the woodpile, it was all circumstantial. She could retract her admission, and since he hadn't given her a Miranda warning, he couldn't use it in court anyway. By the time he arrested her, she could change her story entirely and say she was somewhere completely different. He needed physical evidence. Something like a vehicle part with a serial number that matched her SUV. If he found that, it was a slam dunk.

Del drained the last of his coffee and started his engine. Time to go back to Wynn's house.

§

As he approached the house, Del could see a man in the alley, behind the part he'd taped off the previous night. He screeched to a stop and jumped out.

"Hey you," he yelled. "Get away from there!"

He ran toward the man, immediately noting his frayed shorts and grubby T-shirt. He looked to be in his fifties, and was so skinny he needed a belt to keep his shorts from falling off his nonexistent hips. The man spun around and threw his hands in the air. "No worries, man. Calm down."

Del was annoyed that he was being treated as if he'd pulled his weapon, which he hadn't. "Don't you see the tape? It's there for a reason."

The man shrugged. He looked middle-aged, though his gray, nappy hair implied he was probably older than he looked. Puerto Rican, or from one of the Caribbean islands maybe.

"Jes' tryin' a help a friend." The man said.

Del narrowed his eyes. A friend? Was this man related to the driver? Could it be that Gordy wasn't the driver after all?

"You're trespassing a crime scene. I should arrest you for interfering with an investigation."

"Steady on, dude," the man said. "How can I be trespassing when all I did was walk outside my backyard?"

"Your backyard?"

"Yeah. I'm a friend o' that young lady that got knocked down."

"Who told you it was a young lady? The driver?"

"Huh? Oh, you mean, why I'm a callin' her young? Winona be at least ten years less'n me. That makes her young in my book."

"Winona?"

"Ain't her real name. She just plain ol' Wynn. But I'm a callin' her Winona ever since she moved here. She like it."

"How do you know Wynn?"

The man shook his head, as if Del were simple. "I told you I'm her neighbor. An' she in big trouble. She need all the help she kin get."

Timing Is Everything

"What's your name and where do you live?" Del asked. He'd already interviewed Mrs. Johnson on one side and the neighbor on the other side was still away.

"Donte McDougal, at your service, Sir." The man saluted, and Del wasn't sure whether he was being mocked or not. "Vietnam Vet, PTSD outpatient at Bay Pines VA, lucky owner of that house over there." He pointed across the alley, catty-corner from Wynn's.

Del felt himself soften. "Thank you for your service, Sir," he responded and saw that, in turn, Donte relaxed too.

"You the young fella investigatin' for our girl?" he asked.

Del nodded. "Did you see anything last night?"

Donte shook his head. "Nah. Wouldn't ya know—I was at the sleep disorders clinic. If I'd a been here for sure I'd a heard something. I'm up till all hours, and noises set off my PTSD. I'd a been out here like a shot if I heard that boom. That's why I was so upset when I got home and old Mrs. J. told me what happened. Marched myself straight down to see our Winona."

Del felt frustrated. Donte might have been the ideal witness if only he'd been here. "I appreciate you wanting to help your neighbor, but you can't trespass on this scene."

"She more than a neighbor, she a friend. That's what we do here, look out for each other. I cut her trees, she cooks me meals."

"Still, you can't be messing with evidence."

"Like this, you mean?" Donte untucked his T-shirt from his shorts and held out a piece of metal.

Del grabbed it and grinned.

§

How much luckier could he be? Forensics had quickly found a serial number matching Gordy's SUV, proving that this was indeed the alley she'd driven up and the woodpile she had plowed into. It was time to make the arrest. Gordy had told him she worked for two nursing homes, and he certainly didn't want to upset the old ladies by showing up there. On the other hand, he didn't want to wait any longer than he had to. In case she was still home, he drove over to Gordy's apartment, but nobody answered the door. He'd have to go to the nursing home. To make it easier on the residents, he decided to call Gordy and tell her to meet him outside the main entrance. He punched the numbers into his phone, but when the Pelican Manor receptionist answered, she said Gordy had called in sick.

A knot formed in his stomach. Not at home and not at work. He looked at his watch. Would her kid still be in school? He called the elementary school and was informed that Sammy Lotan's mother had called him out sick that morning.

Was it a coincidence or had she fled? And if she had, where the hell had she run to? If she'd picked up her SUV and wanted to drive to Mexico, he had plenty of time to alert the authorities. But what if she'd jumped on a plane that morning? Del hoped with every fiber of his being that wasn't the case. He wanted to help Wynn, and he wanted to help his career. A suspect who'd fled the country would do neither.

CHAPTER TWENTY

Wynn

"Do you want the good news or the bad news?"
Wynn sat up in her hospital bed and rolled her eyes. What was it with all these professionals that they thought this was an appropriate way of talking to people? First the doctor, now the police officer.
"Oh for chrissake, just tell me what's going on." She hated sounding so grumpy. It didn't suit her. But nor did lying in a hospital bed, incapacitated.
Officer Delgado's expression switched from excited to crestfallen.
"I'm sorry," Wynn said. "I just really need to get things sorted out. Most of all I need you to find the guy who did it. If he owned an SUV that fancy, I'm presuming he had good insurance. And I'm gonna need to make a really big claim. I've already had the hospital financial people hounding me. I'm going to lose all my regular income from not doing my jewelry, and it sounds like I'll need to pay for a ton of home health care. So unless we find this guy, I'm gonna be broke."
"Mom," Tina interjected. "I told you. I'm going to take a break from college. Stop worrying about all that." Tina was sitting by her bedside, stroking her arm. What a godsend that girl had been. But Wynn wasn't having it.
"Like I said, I'll need to pay for home health care while my

daughter returns to college." She glared at Tina. "So please . . . the only good news is that you found him. Anything else is bad news."

"In that case, I definitely have good news for you. But—"

"You found him? Oh! I want to hug you right now." Wynn looked uselessly at her arms, still extended in various contraptions in front of her. "Who is he?"

"He's a she, but that's not important. What's important is—"

"A woman?" She was disappointed.

Tina turned to face her. "Oh for god's sake, Mom, don't be so naive. She's probably some druggie, like all the women my birth mom hangs out with." Tina's face was twisted as she said the words, and Wynn could see she must be flashing back to some of those times when she was small and the police burst in to arrest her mother. Sometimes she almost forgot how Tina and Mikki started their lives. It had been a big step for Tina's birth mom to give up her parental rights. She'd done it because she knew it was for the best, even though she was determined to stay clean and sober. And she did—but only for a few weeks. That was the point at which Tina had decided to cut all contact with her. Anything else was too painful. She rarely even mentioned her birth mom these days.

"So some bitch plowed into my mom and ran off. Have you arrested her?" Tina jumped out of her chair and stood glaring at the officer.

"Not yet. But after I interviewed her yesterday, I knew she was definitely the driver."

"She admitted it?" Wynn asked. She'd been surprised to hear the driver was a woman, and now she was even more shocked to hear that this woman had fessed up. If she was the type to drive away from the scene of a crime, why would she cooperate with the police?

"No. I didn't ask her to. I saw her vehicle at an auto repair shop yesterday so I went to her home. I told her I just needed to rule her out of a hit-and-run, and she said right away that she'd driven up an alley and crashed into something. She thought it was just the woodpile that damaged her car."

"Oh . . ." Wynn's voice was barely a whisper. "She didn't know?"

Tina turned toward her fiercely. "Don't start making excuses for her! If she'd had the decency to get out of the car, she'd have known." She turned back to the officer. "So why didn't you arrest her?"

"I needed definitive proof. Something that tied her vehicle to the accident. I didn't have it last night, so for the time being I told her not to leave town."

"You told her not to leave town." Tina's tone was a heavy mix of sarcasm and disbelief. "You warned her?" She shoved her hands on her hips, her elbows sticking out aggressively. "Why the heck would you do that?"

"She's a nice lady with a cute kid. She didn't strike me as a flight risk."

Tina shook her head from side to side in disbelief and Wynn wondered if she was thinking of all the times her mom had been with a kid and no one had ever given her the benefit of the doubt. Tina had seen her mom arrested so many times that by the end she'd kept a backpack ready in case she got pulled out of the home.

Wynn turned to Officer Delgado. "You said you didn't have proof last night. Do you now?"

"Yes. Before I went to work this morning I searched the alley and found a piece of her vehicle."

"You're sure it's hers?"

"Positive."

"So why aren't you at her house, arresting her?" Tina was still standing, hands on hips, glaring at the officer.

The officer looked sheepish. "I'm sorry to say, this is the not-so-good news. She's not at home or at work, and her son didn't go to school today either."

"I knew it!" Tina yelled. "Let's put on the fucking kid gloves before we arrest a 'nice'"—she made air quotes with her fingers and her tone was thick with sarcasm—"lady with a 'nice' kid. In fact, let's go one step further. Let's tell her not to leave town, which is another way of saying, you better get out of here while you can." Tina turned on him with a vicious look in her eyes. "What was it? Did she bat her eyelashes at you? Or maybe she's Hispanic and Senor Delgado didn't want to lock up one of —"

"Stop it!" Wynn interjected. "That's enough." But she couldn't help noticing Officer Delgado's face had turned red. Had Tina hit close to home with something she said?

"Fucking incompetence . . ." Tina continued to mutter. Wynn wished she could put her hand on her daughter's arm. She would have wanted to calm her down, and at the same time show that she understood. But her arm was stuck out in front of her in that wretched contraption.

"So, now what?" Wynn knew her voice sounded thin and reedy, like an old woman's. And right now, she felt old. When Officer Delgado said they'd found the driver, she'd thought her luck was changing, but now she just felt tired.

"We'll find her," the officer said. Wynn wished she could hear confidence in his voice, but she wasn't sure even he believed what he was saying. "She picked up her car from the auto mechanic, who says he has no idea where she was headed, but I'm not convinced he's telling the truth. We do know she didn't leave it at the airport and didn't take any flights, so she must be driving somewhere. We know her license plate number, and we can track her cell phone. She has a child with her, so that makes fleeing even harder." He turned toward the door. "I'll keep you posted," he said. "I promise."

"Thanks," Wynn said weakly. She supposed it was still better knowing who the driver was than not knowing, even if the woman had skipped town.

As Officer Delgado left, he stood aside to let someone else come in. Wynn wondered which nurse or aide it was this time, probably wanting to take her blood pressure or ply her with pills.

"Hi honey." It was Kat, loaded down with a bunch of wildflowers and a bag of purple grapes which she put by the bedside. "Anything new?"

"They found her!" Wynn said at the same time as Tina said, "They lost her!"

"Who?" Kat's face had a look of complete confusion.

"The driver." Wynn said. "They know who it is. Only, when they went to arrest her, she'd fled."

"But listen to this!" Tina interjected. "The assholes warned her. They went to her home last night, interviewed her, then told her not to leave town. Isn't that like telling someone not to scratch their nose? I mean, who does that?"

"It wasn't quite like that," Wynn said. When Tina wasn't around, Wynn felt pretty riled up about everything. But when Tina expressed so much anger, Wynn found herself wanting to be the one who calmed things down. "Tina, why don't you go get some fresh air. I need a few minutes with Kat."

Tina looked from one to the other. She bent over Wynn and

kissed her gently on the cheek. "I'll be right back."

"She's a funny one, isn't she?" Kat said, after Tina closed the door behind her. "Furious one second, and so gentle the next."

Wynn nodded. "Best thing that ever happened to me. I mean, Mikki's wonderful too, but she's never had that same intensity Tina has."

"Is she right? Are they messing up the investigation?"

Wynn sighed. "I'm not sure. He says he's doing everything he can, but . . ." She trailed off. Wynn had her reasons for not fully trusting law enforcement, but she'd never shared them with Kat. Kat didn't even know Wynn had once been under arrest or what had happened with Barker. She supposed at some point she'd share the whole story with her, but now wasn't the time.

"I understand," Kat said, a far-off look in her eyes. She took a plastic cup from the top of Wynn's cupboard, filled it with water, and then began arranging the wildflowers.

Wynn watched her and thought about what a good friend she'd become over the past few months. "I have to ask you a favor," she said, and Kat turned around to face her. "I need someone on my side to get involved with this investigation. Tina would do it, but you've seen how she is. She's too emotional about everything. I need a levelheaded person to make sure this cop doesn't drop the baton."

"I'm ahead of you. I already asked my friend Carrie Ann who works at the Town Hall about him. She said he's a good guy, a hard worker."

"He probably is. But I don't know. Something Tina said . . . the way he reacted. Almost as if he wanted that driver to get away. I don't know if it's true, but I do know that he seems to be doing this whole investigation by himself. Why hasn't he pulled in his colleagues? Is he trying to be some kind of hero and solve the whole case on his own?"

Kat laughed. "Sweetie, that completely contradicts what you just said about him letting the driver get away."

"I suppose it does. I guess I'm not making sense. The thing is, I'm so worried I can't think straight. I haven't let the girls know how bad it is, but I may be really screwed financially, unless I can claim on that driver's insurance. I know you're still in the throes of a budding honeymoon romance, but will you help me?"

"Of course. Even better—Gabriella can help you too. She's

going to be staying with me for a while."

Wynn was shocked. "She's moving in already? What about her son? You told me you hadn't even met him yet."

"I'll meet him tonight. And it's not exactly moving in . . ." Kat's face took on a small frown. "Tell me how we can help you."

"Can you look in the alley behind the house and see if there's more evidence they might have missed?"

"When I took the dogs out yesterday, I saw that the area where you were knocked down is all taped off."

"There's a gate in my back fence. We never use it, because the mango tree got so big it's awkward to get to, but you could slip out of the yard into the alley from there. No-one would see you."

"Then I will. And better yet," Kat's eyes were filled with excitement, "I can enlist Gabriella's son to help me. Make it a game of hide and seek. He'll love that."

"No," Wynn said. "It's not a game." It sounded sharper than she'd intended. "I mean, don't say anything to Gabriella or her kid right now. This is just between you and me. Okay?"

"I don't like keeping secrets from Gordy. It's not a good way to start."

"Gordy?"

"It's her nickname for friends and family. She told me right away that she wanted me to use it. There's something really special between us. That's why I wanted to share this with her."

"I know. But for right now, I just . . ." Her voice trailed off. She was too tired to explain. "Please?"

"You're going through a lot." Kat patted the bed. "I'm sorry."

"Maybe you could also try to figure out where the heck the driver's fled to. People might not want to talk to the police, but they'll talk to you. If Officer Delgado will give you a name . . . "

The door opened. Tina was back. "Time's up," she said to Kat. "Mom needs to rest. The doctor told me to keep everyone's visits short and sweet."

Kat bent over and pushed a strand of hair off Wynn's face. "Hang in there," she said, then straightened up and looked suspiciously at Tina. "Have you eaten today?"

"I . . ." Tina looked at her feet.

"You haven't, have you?" Tina didn't answer. "Come on," Kat said, linking her arm in Tina's. "I'm going to take you home to meet Gordy, and then you're going to entertain her son while

Gordy helps me cook us all a delicious dinner."

Tina promised she'd come back to say goodnight, and Wynn watched with envy as the two of them walked away. Kat's homemade dinners were to die for. Not only would Tina get to enjoy an amazing meal, she'd also get to meet Gabriella Luna, the woman who had stolen Kat's heart. Wynn felt her jealousy intensify, like a handful of thorns pricking her chest. If only Wynn could spend the evening with them too. But she was stuck in this damn bed and would shortly be brought some sort of mushy mess on a plate that a nurse's aide would shove into her mouth too quickly while he looked at his watch and wondered how much time was left on his shift. Wynn felt tears form in her eyes, then felt a burst of anger when she remembered she couldn't even brush them aside.

She took a deep breath and reminded herself that she had people on her side. There was Officer Delgado and, even if Tina returned to school, she still had Kat. Between them, they'd find that driver and make sure she got what was coming to her. Someone would know her and have ideas about where she would have fled. You couldn't keep secrets in a small place like Gulfport.

CHAPTER TWENTY-ONE

Gabriella

"Why didn't I go to school today, Mami?" Sammy asked, as he looked up from his Legos.

Gordy barely heard him. She was absorbed with the material she was reading on her laptop. It wasn't good. Just as she'd thought, the latest governmental pronouncements said that immigrants involved in unresolved cases could be deported. But what did "unresolved" mean? She posted a question anonymously on one of the legal websites and got a quick answer back.

We don't know what they mean by unresolved. They haven't specified. We'd like to think they would wait until someone's received due legal process, but we can't be sure. If you need legal representation, please contact us at . . .

"Will I go to school tomorrow, Mamita?"

"I . . . I'm not sure."

It was a mess. She'd pulled Sammy out of school without thinking. She hadn't contacted Dana, but she was going to have to tell her ex something soon and she had no idea how she would react. When they'd decided to separate, Dana had reassured Gordy that she would never do anything to obstruct her path to citizenship. They both agreed that their coparenting would always revolve around what was best for Sammy. But they didn't always agree on what that was. Dana was a strict parent who thought kids flourished best when there were clear rules for them to follow. Gordy agreed that rules were important, but also believed they were made to be broken. She thought parents should be flexible, even after they'd made a rule or a decision. Dana thought that was just an excuse to let Sammy walk all over her. Gordy's parents had encouraged her to be independent from a young age, and she was convinced it was what had given her the confidence to leave her homeland and relocate to the USA. Gordy wanted to give Sammy that same sense of independence and confidence, so she allowed him to make decisions, even when they were bad ones.

"That's how he'll learn to be responsible and make a better choice next time," she'd told Dana when Sammy threw up after eating way too much candy on Halloween.

"Yeah, right. What if he ate something that gave him food poisoning? Kids can't make responsible decisions. That's why parents do it on their behalf."

"But that's the whole point. He won't learn to make those decisions unless we give him the opportunity. By seeing the results of his overindulging he'll learn how to restrain himself."

"Or not. Maybe he'll just learn that it's okay to do whatever you want. Next thing you know, he'll be in college and get alcohol poisoning when he drinks too much."

"Not if we teach him moderation. In Mexico we let the kids have a little beer or tequila at family celebrations and fiestas so they can learn how to appreciate alcohol instead of overindulging because it's forbidden."

"You're not in Mexico now," Dana snarled, "and it's not gonna happen on my watch."

Their differing parenting styles still came up whenever there was some sort of joint decision to be made. Despite the arguments, or maybe because of them, Gordy knew that sometimes she was wrong. Now was one of those times. She'd acted spontaneously, pulling Sammy out of school without thinking how it might affect him. She'd been sure she was going to bundle him in their car and head for the border, but it had been a stupid idea. Whatever was going to happen, Sammy needed to live his life as normally as possible. Tomorrow he had to go back to school.

But she couldn't be the one to take him. That cop had told her not to leave town and if he had any intention of arresting her, the school would be one of the first places he'd search for her. Dana would have to take Sammy to school, which meant that she would have to take Sammy to Dana. Once she did that, Dana would know her whereabouts and would feel obligated to tell the police if they came looking for her. Even though Dana knew it wasn't in Sammy's best interests for Gordy to be arrested, she was one of the most law-abiding people Gordy knew. There was no way she wouldn't tell the truth, and Gordy couldn't ask her to lie.

She wished she hadn't brought Sammy to Kat's. It would have been better if he didn't know where his mother was, in case anyone asked him. But did he know? She tried to remember what she'd told him when she put the key in the lock of Kat's house and opened the door for them.

"How come you have her key?"

"Because she's a very dear friend who—"

"Then why haven't I met her?"

"You will. Tonight. Mami has some work to do. Will you play with your Legos?"

She hadn't even said Kat's name, and he certainly wasn't aware enough to know what neighborhood he was in. What if she took him over to Dana's right now and told them both she was leaving town? She could tell them an emergency had come up and she had to go to Mexico.

"Look, Mami!" Sammy pulled on her shorts, so that she could admire the complicated sky tower he was creating with his Legos. She bent down and swept him into her arms.

"It's fantastic," she said. He smelled of the apple juice he'd been drinking. She squeezed him tight. She couldn't bear the thought of leaving him without knowing when she might see him again. She had been so sure she wasn't responsible for that hit-and-run, but now her certainty was eroding. She buried her face in Sammy's curly hair, then started planting kisses all over his face. "I love you so much, Sammy, *yo te quiero tanto.*" Her throat was tight and she felt tears starting to prick her eyes.

"Eeeow!" He wriggled out of her grasp and slid to the floor. He sat in front of the sky tower and looked toward the remaining pieces of Lego scattered on the floor.

"Shall I make something else? I can knock this one down." He looked up at Gordy as he said it, and a look of concern swept his little face. "Don't cry, Mamita. I'll keep it the way it is. I can read my book for school instead."

He stood up and marched toward his schoolbag. She brushed the tears from her face. She had to be strong. Crying wasn't going to help. Nor was keeping Sammy out of school. She might need to lay low, but her child didn't. She would take him to Dana's and tell them she was leaving town. Then she would come back to Kat's and tell her everything. She would ask Kat to find out as much as she could about the hit-and-run accident described in the *Gazette*. Kat knew almost everyone in town. Maybe she could find out who the victim was and get information the police didn't have, proving it wasn't her. Possibly, she'd overreacted and really wasn't the prime suspect. Perhaps by now they'd already found another bashed-in car and another driver and she was worrying over nothing. When the cop told her not to leave town, it could have just been because it was something he told everyone.

But what if it wasn't? What if they knew it was her and had no intention of looking for anyone else? If only she'd spent a couple of minutes longer checking the entire alley. She'd swept her flashlight across the area, but she'd done it not expecting to see anything unusual. As soon as she saw the woodpile and the fallen logs, she'd been sure that was what she'd hit. Had she really looked any further? Up until today it never even occurred to her that she could have hit a person, but now . . . She took a deep breath. She knew what she had to do. She'd take Sammy over to Dana's, and after that she'd keep her SUV safely parked inside Kat's garage.

She messaged Dana. *Okay if I bring Sammy a day early? Family emergency. Need to leave town.*

She was relieved when a message came back a few seconds later. *Sure. Hope everyone's okay.*

CHAPTER TWENTY-TWO

Kat

Kat rang her doorbell and waited for Gordy to answer. It felt odd to stand outside her own front door, but she'd given Gordy the key she always used and the spare one was tucked away in a desk drawer. She waited but nobody answered.

She rang again. Still no answer. She pressed her ear against the door, but heard nothing. A momentary doubt assailed her. She had given her house key to Gordy without thinking twice about it. Yet she'd barely known this woman a month. This was the same woman who just that morning had tried to give her a burner phone and skip town because she was being accused of a crime. Kat had no idea what the crime was, but the word felony had been used. Suppose it was burglary or larceny and Gordy had decided to have one more spree before taking off for good? What if everything Gordy had ever told Kat was a lie? Maybe there was no kid. Maybe Gordy had seen her as an easy target that first night at The Dive and had planned to rob her all along. She shook her head at how ridiculous she was being. After a couple of days with Kat, Gordy would have known she'd made a poor choice if she was in it for the money. Kat's computer was years old, she didn't own any jewelry, and what little cash she had to her name was safely in the bank. She heard a plaintive meow and smiled, despite herself. If Gordy had cleaned her out, at least she'd left Pnina behind.

She rapped hard on the door. "Gordy? Are you there?"

Immediately some rustling and then the door was flung open.

"I'm sorry," Gordy's hand was on her chest as if she were trying to calm it down. "I got scared. I didn't know who was at the door. I forgot that the key you gave me was off your key ring." She pulled Kat indoors and closed the door quickly.

Kat looked around and saw a single suitcase standing neatly against the wall with Gordy's briefcase stacked against it. No sign of a child, a child's clothes, or any toys. "Where's Sammy?"

"I took him to Dana's."

"I thought—"

"It's a long story. I'll tell you the whole thing over dinner. I wanted to cook you a nice meal, even though the idea of cooking for a chef is scary. But when I looked in your pantry, I didn't find much. Not in your fridge either."

Kat smiled ruefully. "Don't you know the shoemaker always goes barefoot? After a day of preparing food for other people, I never cook for myself." She placed a bag of groceries on the countertop. "But I went to the store on the way home because today you and I are going to cook together. I—" She was about to tell her Tina was coming over after walking the dogs but Gordy pulled her close, grabbing her into a big hug.

"I love you, Katya Ayalon. You have no idea how much this means to me. Being here . . ." She trailed off and a frown appeared between her eyes.

"Don't worry. It's all gonna work out. Whatever *it* is. Kiss me," she commanded, and Gordy obliged with a passion that surprised Kat with its ferocity. Reluctantly she pulled away.

"Let's have a beer," she said, moving toward the fridge. "We'll sit on the front patio, and you can tell me exactly what's going on."

"The back porch," Gordy said as she took a bottle from Kat. "Nobody can see us there."

Kat couldn't believe how scared Gordy seemed. Whatever this was about must be serious. The crazy thoughts she'd had a few minutes earlier returned. Had she been in denial when Gordy showed her a burner phone and said she was skipping town? Was Gordy someone entirely different from the person she appeared to be? Kat felt her stomach clench and realized she was flashing back to last year when she'd been involved with a woman who turned out to be housing very dark secrets. Surely it couldn't happen twice? Was there something about her that screamed *"sucker!"* to these people? As she walked toward the back porch, clutching the ice-cold bottle in her hand, Kat tried to think if there were red flags she had missed as she got to know Gordy.

The first night they met, she'd been amazed at their similarities. Now she wondered: was it really coincidence? Had Gordy somehow done her homework on Kat? She raked through her mind for other red flags. She'd never been to Gordy's home. Gordy had told her it was because of Sammy, but even her friends questioned that. She'd accepted that it wasn't yet appropriate for her to go because of Gordy's son, but what if Sammy didn't even exist? She shook her head. It was crazy thinking. Gordy had shown her endless pictures on her phone of herself with a curly haired kid. But that didn't prove it was her son. He could be her nephew or a friend's kid, or the images could have been photoshopped.

Kat stood in the doorway and watched Gordy kick off her shoes and take a seat on the double hammock where she and Gordy had lazed blissfully several times over the past few weeks, describing their childhoods to each other, marveling at their similarities and reveling in some of their differences. Just a few days ago as they swung together they'd begun to plan a future vacation. A camping trip to the Keys, snorkeling, maybe even scuba diving. It had all felt perfect. Too perfect?

"You're not going to sit next to me?" Gordy asked her. She broke from her reverie and realized that she was still rooted to her spot in the doorway.

"Of course," she said and plunked herself down next to Gordy. "But tell me what's going on. I can't wait any longer."

"Earlier today I asked you if you trust me. You said you did and invited me to stay here. But . . . I'm watching you and something feels different. Did something happen this afternoon?"

"No." Kat paused. She turned to Gordy. "I'm just a little freaked out by the way you're acting. You brought a burner phone to my work. You said you were going to skip town. You don't want anyone to see you here. It makes me nervous."

"I must look like a crazy woman to you." The corners of Gordy's mouth turned down in a grimace. "If I weren't so scared about immigration, I wouldn't be acting this way. I'm not the kind of person who won't face things, however hard they are. I don't think I did what they're accusing me of, but—"

"Wait! You don't *think* you did? What does that mean?"

Timing Is Everything

Gordy took Kat's hands in her own and faced her directly. "Listen. The other night when I left you I was running late."

"I know. You ran out on me. Not quite the same way as our first meeting. This time you at least told me why you had to run."

"Right. Well, I made a stupid mistake. Dana texted me. She was mad that I wasn't there to pick up Sammy. She threatened to put him out on the street."

"Ms. Super Responsibility would do that?"

Gordy shook her head. "I know she wouldn't have. But I panicked. I decided to send Dana a quick text to tell her I was on my way. And that's what started this whole mess."

"I don't know much about the law, but if the cops saw you texting, that can't be serious enough to get deported."

"I wish that was what had happened. While I was texting I had an accident. That's why my car was in the shop."

Gordy was still grasping Kat's hands in hers. Now Kat pulled them away. "Cut to the chase. What aren't you telling me? An accident's an accident. What's the big bad thing that could get you deported?"

"An old lady got knocked down and the driver took off."

Jeez. First Wynn, and now some poor old lady. What was going on in Gulfport? Maybe it was the same driver who hit them both.

"And you didn't do it," Kat said.

"No."

"Then I don't see what the problem is. You'll prove your innocence just like anyone else who has to prove the cops got the wrong person."

"No! It's not just like everyone else. Remember how ecstatic I was that I had my biometrics appointment coming up? Well, now I wish to heavens I didn't. If I didn't have a current application in the system, no one would be checking up on me right now. By the time Immigration found out about the arrest, I'd already have been cleared of all charges. But this is the worst possible time an arrest could happen. If they charge me with a felony, it will take a while to go through the system. Nothing will be resolved quickly. But in a week, I go to USCIS to be fingerprinted. It's the final time they'll check my criminal background. So what will they see? That I'm currently under arrest. That's why I'm so worried."

Kat felt confused. "But all they'll see is an arrest. It won't show you've been convicted."

"It doesn't matter." Gordy raised her voice a little, as if that would help Kat understand. "The person reviewing the file has to judge it based on what's in front of them. Can you imagine if they approved it and then I turned out to be a major criminal? Nobody's going to approve a file with an active arrest on it."

"So then, they would just put it on hold until they had the final outcome of your case, wouldn't they?"

"Are you kidding? Immigration is swamped. Some of their offices are literally years behind on their paperwork. If they started putting cases on hold, things would be even messier than they are already. No, whoever is responsible for approving my application makes one decision. Yes or No."

Kat finally began to see why Gordy was so worried. It didn't sound fair, but maybe she was right.

"What happens if they don't approve it? Do you have to file over again?"

"No. Once I'm turned down, I'm no longer legal and I have to leave the country."

The doorbell rang and Gordy immediately looked alarmed, shrinking into her chair as if ICE were already here to grab her.

"Don't worry. That's my friend Wynn's daughter, Tina. Wynn's in the hospital so I invited her over to dinner."

"But I thought—"

"Don't panic! It's just dinner. Wynn's a good friend, and Tina's a good kid." She turned around and yelled in the direction of the front door. "It's open. Come on in."

Kat got up and went to greet Tina. Kat could see she'd made an effort to clean up. She'd changed out of khaki cargo pants into navy ones, and had put on a clean, albeit baggy, T-shirt advertising an all-girl band. Kat smiled to herself. Tina was a young butch if ever there was one. Kat handed her a soda and led her to the back porch where she made the introductions. She watched as Tina looked Gordy up and down, from the lustrous hair to her ample bosom and curvy hips. Tina glanced toward Kat and grinned a smile of approval.

"Everything okay with the dogs?" Kat asked, embarrassed and pleased at the same time.

Tina nodded. "They were so happy to be let out, I think they took me for a walk instead of me taking them." She looked around.

"Where's the kid I'm meant to be babysitting?"

"My son?" asked Gordy, as she pulled herself a little taller in her chair. "I took him to his other mother."

Kat intimated the hammock to Tina. "Why don't you chill out while we make dinner. You've had a long day, and Gordy and I have a conversation we need to finish."

In the kitchen, Kat pulled onions and peppers out of her shopping bag and gave them to Gordy along with a chopping knife.

"So, this accident," she said. "Why do they think you're the driver? What proof do they have?"

"I don't know. I think maybe my SUV matched the vehicle description the old lady gave them. A cop went to my cousin's auto shop, and when he saw my vehicle he asked for my address. Then he came to interview me."

"But he didn't arrest you."

"No. He said he was ruling people out, and at first I thought I'd satisfied whatever concern he had. But then something changed, and before he left he told me not to leave town."

"I talked to you yesterday and you never said anything."

"I didn't think it was a big deal. Until this morning. I was taking Sammy to school and I got scared. Started to think that the moment I arrived at work I was going to be arrested. So I took Sammy home, picked up the car, and bought that stupid burner phone."

Kat took the chopped vegetables from Gordy and threw them in a pan. She tossed in pasta, garlic, and spices and began stirring it all together. She was trying to take in what Gordy had told her, but something wasn't making sense. She threw in some wine and decided to focus on her cooking. Perhaps it was because she was hungry that she couldn't think straight.

"Let's set the table. We can talk about this more later."

It turned out they were all so hungry that once the food was on the table, they were too busy eating to make conversation. After they'd scraped the pasta bowl clean, Kat spooned gelato into small glass dishes.

"Tell Gordy about your future tennis career, Tina. She's a tennis fan too."

Tina shrugged. "I'm good, but there are plenty who are way

better. Don't tell Mom, but I'm thinking of not going back to college. I could get a job at the tennis club in town and play a whole lot more tennis than I have time for now with all my studies."

"She'd kill you!" Kat said. "Do you know how much and how often she boasts about having two daughters in college?" She didn't add, *and about how much you've overcome to even get there.*

"Right now she's not in a position to do much of anything," Tina muttered.

"If it's not too personal, may I ask why your Mom's in hospital?" Gordy asked.

"She was in an accident. Broken arms, hips, internal stuff."

"That's terrible. I'm so sorry."

"Not as sorry as the driver's gonna be when we track her down. Mom was putting out the garbage in the alley and some asshole drove into her, then drove away without stopping. And yeah, before you ask, it's a woman."

Kat had heard of people who turned pale. Usually people threw in banal references, like white as a sheet. But looking at Gordy, she knew the description wasn't accurate. Gordy had lost so much color it was as if her skin had disappeared altogether, its healthy latte sheen transformed into a sickly gray that made her eyes appear hollow and her mouth too large for her face. Or maybe that was because it was open and she was gasping. Kat watched, puzzled, and then all of a sudden she felt a chasm open up in the pit of her stomach. She knew why Gordy was reacting that way. Kat felt light-headed, as if the blood was being drained out of her veins. She wanted to extract the thought that was suddenly pulsing to the front of her brain and destroy it, but it was lodged there.

"When you track down the driver?" Gordy's voice cracked as she spoke.

"Yeah. The bitch skipped town. Can you imagine? First you run over someone and leave them injured on the ground. And then, when you realize the cops are onto you, you just flee. Would you do that?"

Tina was spooning gelato into her mouth. Nobody answered. Tina looked from one to the other. "I'm sorry, guys. I know I come on too heavy. I'm just upset about Mom. I didn't mean to imply either of you would ever do that. I'm an idiot."

Kat knew she had to say something, but she couldn't think

what. Could Gordy be the driver who put Wynn in the hospital? When she said she was a suspect in knocking down an old lady Kat had pictured some feeble crone bent over a walker who was knocked down as she tried to cross the street. Wynn was in her sixties. Maybe whoever told Gordy the victim was elderly thought sixty-something was old. Looking at Gordy's ashen face and round eyes, she suspected her lover was coming to the same conclusion.

"Where—where did you say your mom was knocked down?"

"The alley by her house. She wasn't just knocked onto the ground. Her friend Donte had trimmed her mango tree and left a bunch of branches piled against her fence. When the car that hit her zoomed by, it knocked her into the woodpile. She's so banged up it's gonna take her months to recover."

There was a moment of silence and then Gordy spoke, her voice barely above a whisper. "Maybe," she said, "the driver didn't know she ran your mom over."

That was it. The thing that hadn't made sense earlier. Gordy had said she wasn't sure she'd committed the crime. Kat had wondered how that could be possible.

"How could the driver not know?" Kat asked, trying not to look directly at Gordy.

"Right?" Tina said. "She must have known she hit something. So either she stopped, saw Mom and drove away, or she just kept going. Either way she's a revolting piece of—"

"Maybe she thought she just hit a pile of wood," Gordy said.

"If she'd taken the time to check it out, she'd have seen my mom, and heard her too. She was probably only unconscious for a minute."

"Why do you keep saying 'she' about the driver?" Gordy's voice was still weak, almost as if she already knew the answer Tina was going to give.

"Because at the hospital Officer Delgado, the investigator, told us he knew who the driver was. He found her car in a repair shop. He interviewed her yesterday but couldn't arrest her because he had no physical proof. This morning he got the proof he needed so he went to arrest her. And surprise—she'd fled."

"Oh . . ." Gordy's face crumpled and she gripped the side of the table.

"I know, right? You know why she left? That moron detective gave her a heads up. Told her yesterday not to skip town."

Kat watched as Gordy put her hands to her face. She felt as if her whole world was spinning in slow motion. They'd both heard what Tina said and had put it together. Gordy was the driver who had knocked Wynn down. It was unthinkable. Unbearable. And yet even from the small amount Gordy had told her about the accident, it had to be true. Gordy clearly thought so. Kat suspected that if she asked her for more details about where she'd been when she texted Dana, there could be no other conclusion.

If only Gordy had stopped and taken care of Wynn. If the alley had been dark and Wynn couldn't be seen, Gordy might not even have been prosecuted. It could have been an honest mistake, like that girl last year who killed a pedestrian and everyone made a fuss because she was never arrested. But from what Tina was saying, the driver hadn't stopped. From the few TV shows she watched, Kat knew that fleeing the scene of a crime was almost worse than committing it in the first place. No wonder Gordy was scared of being deported.

Kat's stomach was roiling and her chest felt so tight she could barely breathe. If she knew Gordy was the driver, wasn't she obligated to tell Wynn and Officer Delgado? But if she did, Gordy would be taken away. If Gordy went to prison or was deported, Kat would lose her and so would Sammy. It wasn't fair. She knew Gordy well enough to know she could never have done something like this on purpose. But she also knew that the law was far harder on people who weren't yet citizens. The local police might want to be lenient with her, but ICE was a different story.

If she said nothing, could she live with herself? She'd promised to help Wynn find the driver. It was what would bring her friend not only peace of mind, but some level of financial security. She knew she wasn't the only one who wanted to help Wynn, but turning her back would be a whole different story. There would be others who would step in, for sure. Gulfport was a small town where everyone looked out for one another. Neighbors brought food over if someone was sick. They tidied storm debris together when winds and rains flooded the streets and left mud and downed branches everywhere. When petty crimes happened, like someone's gardening tools being taken from their front yard, they banded together, sending flurries of texts and Facebook posts until someone spotted the missing shears or pruners. They would be there for Wynn because there was no way they would let anyone get away with committing a major crime. It wasn't who they were. But breaking a promise to her friend wasn't who she was either.

Tina had finished her gelato and was sitting back, her hands interlaced across the back of her head, her elbows to the sides, a young girl who'd stopped worrying about her injured mom long enough to enjoy a delicious meal in the company of close friends. She's oblivious, Kat thought. If only I were. She couldn't look at Gordy, whose face was still buried in her hands. Instead, she looked out beyond the patio at the Spanish moss draped over the live oak making the tree look like a widow veiled in mourning.

She heard a cough and turned to see that Gordy had taken her hands away from her face and was now facing Tina directly.

"Tina." Gordy's voice was slow and deliberate. It was so husky that for a moment Kat was overcome with longing for the Gordy she had met just over a month ago, the fun, playful, sexual woman she wanted to spend the rest of her life with. But there was nothing romantic about Gordy's words. In fact, Kat was aghast when she heard them.

Gordy's voice was quiet, but resolved. "There's something I have to tell you."

Alison R. Solomon

PART TWO

KAT

CHAPTER TWENTY-THREE

"Tina." Gordy said. "There's something I have to tell you."

She was making the decision for me. While I'd been frantically racking my brain trying to figure out what to do, she'd been doing the same.

"No! No you don't." I said.

I had to stop her. Gordy was going to tell Tina she was the driver, and I couldn't let her. It was one thing for someone—even someone like me—to accuse Gordy or to suggest it might be her. It was quite another for her to confess it herself. She'd told me that just being accused of a crime could be bad enough for her to lose her status here. I was terrified that if she openly admitted it then for sure she'd be deported. They probably wouldn't even bother with a trial. Just kick her out and slam the door firmly so she could never come back.

I couldn't let her make any kind of admission. She'd said she wasn't sure it was her and while that seemed far-fetched, if she confessed it would be too late to change her mind or consider any other possibilities. Especially if she admitted it to Wynn's daughter. Tina was hopping mad about what had happened to her mom. She'd hotfoot it to Officer Delgado before Gordy even finished speaking—or maybe she'd stop long enough to lay her out flat on the way out. I didn't know what Gordy's options were, but I did know this wasn't one of them.

Gordy looked startled that I'd stopped her, while Tina looked perplexed.

"Something to tell me?" Tina said. "Are you a lawyer? Or better yet, a private investigator?" Her tone was hopeful.

"No." I interjected. "I think Gordy wanted to tell you that she's had a really long day and she's bushed."

"It didn't sound like that to me. It sounded like you were going to say something about my mom's situation. Were you?"

The sun had gone down and the air was getting cold. All around us crickets rubbed their wings together, a droning Greek chorus reverberating with the buzzing inside my head.

Gordy was looking right at me. I shook my head just enough for her to see but to be imperceptible to Tina.

Gordy's voice was shaky. "I was shocked by what you told me. I—I wanted to tell you that I believe you will find who you're looking for." I nodded ever so slightly, signaling my approval.

"I know I will." Tina said, her hands on her hips. "I won't rest until I do." She was glaring at us, and then her expression softened. "It's really good to know Mom has friends she can trust who are going to help her. We're all in this together aren't we?"

"We certainly are," Gordy said and for a moment I was scared that she was going to try again to make a confession.

Tina scraped her chair back. "I don't want to outstay my welcome. I promised Mom I'd go back to the hospital to say goodnight and to give her an update on the dogs. Thanks for dinner. Delicious as always."

We stayed seated after she left, the silence between us louder than the crickets. Pnina wandered in from the garden, eying Gordy warily. Pnina was a one-woman cat. Although she'd been happy enough to let Cindy feed her, I was always the one she went to for strokes and cuddles. Now, however, she jumped onto Gordy's lap. I smiled to myself, my heart heavy.

"Why?" Gordy said eventually.

"You told me you don't know for sure. Is that true?"

"I didn't know. I really didn't. But after Tina said . . ." Her voice trailed away.

"You told me an old lady got knocked down. That doesn't mean—"

"It must be me."

I was surprised by how sure Gordy sounded. "Tell me the whole story," I said, "including what you left out."

"I was racing back to Dana's. I always go the same way, but there was a U-Haul blocking the street. So I took a side alley. As I told you, I texted Dana to let her know I was coming. The next thing I knew, I felt this tremendous jolt. I realized I'd plowed into something, but I was so intent on getting to Dana's that at first I didn't want to stop. I knew I had to, so I jumped out of the SUV and ran back. I saw a pile of wood and figured that's what I had hit."

"You saw the woodpile. That's why you think it was you. And Wynn? Did you see Wynn?"

"No. Obviously I didn't look hard enough."

"But you'd have heard her groaning."

"I didn't hear anything. I'm sure of it." She paused. "But maybe she was dazed or concussed and didn't make any noise at first. Maybe she only came to after I drove away."

Gordy was right. It probably happened exactly that way. Gordy hadn't seen Wynn so she'd driven off. But did it count as a hit-and-run if the driver didn't know she'd hit somebody? Gordy wasn't some lowlife who knew what she did and tried to flee the scene.

I thought about Wynn. How banged up she was. It was much more than being banged up. She was hurt on every level—physically, emotionally, and financially. Her whole life had been turned upside down. One minute she was happily organizing her business so she could have her best season ever, and the next everything was a disaster. And the woman I loved might be the cause of it all.

"You were going to tell Tina it was you," I said.

"What choice do I have? It's the right thing to do."

"But you'll lose everything. Your home, Sammy, me . . ."

She turned toward me. "You think I don't know this? But even if it weren't the right thing, it's only a matter of time before they figure out where I am. They'll find me, and if they know you were hiding me here, you'll be in trouble too."

Harboring a fugitive was the phrase that came to mind although I had no idea if it applied in this situation. The whole thing was crazy. If her fingerprint appointment had been two weeks earlier, she'd have nothing to worry about. She could have turned herself in and let the chips fall wherever they were headed. She might have been arrested or they might have let her go, believing that she had no idea she'd knocked Wynn over. Either way she wouldn't have had to worry that she'd lose her home and her kid and the country she'd been living in for all these years.

Tina's words were still squawking in my brain. "It's really good to know Mom has friends she can trust who are going to help her."

I wanted to help Wynn. Desperately. She deserved all the help she could get. But I wanted to help the woman I was in love with equally desperately. The problem was that there seemed to be no way I could help one without selling out the other.

CHAPTER TWENTY-FOUR

"I have to turn myself in," Gordy said to my back, as we lay in bed, neither one of us able to sleep.

We'd cleaned up the dishes, pulled the cushions off the patio chairs in case it rained, and closed the blinds. Gordy had left her suitcase stacked in the corner of my bedroom, pulling out only a nightshirt and her wash bag.

"I know." I rolled over to face her and propped myself up on one elbow. With the other hand, I stroked her hair, letting the thick waves undulate through my fingers. "But maybe not just yet."

"What's the point in prolonging it?" She ran the back of her fingers down my cheek.

"Make love to me," I whispered.

"I can't." She pulled her hand away from my face. "How can you think about that at a time like this?"

"Because I'm terrified it might never happen again."

"Oh . . ." Her fingers went back to stroking my cheek. "It's just . . ."

"I know." I wasn't in the mood for sex either. But my mind was spinning forward. She said she was going to turn herself in. She'd go to the police station, confess, get whisked away to some Immigration Detention Center who knows where. And then what? How would I see her again? They probably only let immediate family visit, if they let anyone at all. Maybe Dana would be able to take Sammy, but I was no one.

"Let's get married tomorrow!" It wasn't the way I pictured a wedding, but it would mean I had legal rights to know what was happening to her.

In the half-light I saw her shake her head.

"I mean it. I told you I love you. Why wait?"

"And I told you. Dana and I aren't divorced. We'll get divorced after I get my ten-year card. *If* I get it."

I felt stupid. Of course she'd told me. I was so desperate I couldn't think straight.

I'm so gay I can't even think straight. The silly bumper sticker came to mind and I couldn't even muster up a grin.

"I can't do this." I said, jumping out of bed.

"I understand." Gordy sat up. "I'm sorry. I should never have involved you. I should never have left my house or—"

"No. I mean, I can't just stand by and watch the life of the woman I love get trampled on." Gordy didn't seem like a drama queen. But I couldn't believe the situation was as serious as she made out. I pulled out my tablet. "I'm going to start my research right now."

It didn't take me long to learn that because Wynn had been injured, and because Gordy had fled the scene, this could well be classified as a felony hit-and-run. And all the links I clicked showed how easy it was to deport noncitizens for felony offenses. But I also learned that sometimes a hit-and-run could be classified as a misdemeanor. If we got her a really good lawyer, maybe they could make the case for a lesser charge, especially since Gordy said she *had* stopped at the scene of the accident. As I read further, I realized that even if we got over that obstacle, there was another one. Wynn could sue Gordy for thousands of dollars of damages, and in Florida damages could be tripled just to further punish the offender. Gordy would be broke for life.

But it wasn't just about Gordy being broke. Wynn was going to be broke if she couldn't get some help. Not just broke but broken. I couldn't support my lover at the expense of my best friend. Yet I couldn't support my best friend if it meant ruining my girlfriend.

Gordy sat next to me, looking over my shoulder and shaking her head.

"I've read it all already. It's why I got so scared. Maybe I'll get lucky. My appointment will get postponed. It happens all the time.

If I don't have an appointment, nobody's going to be checking up on me."

"What difference does it make? If they arrest you and we can't get all the charges removed, you might have to go to prison, and once that happens it won't make any difference what status your green card is."

"But I don't think I have a choice. I have to do the right thing."

I felt as if a vise were pressing my head, squeezing my temples. If that was my experience, I couldn't imagine how Gordy must be feeling. However bad it was for me, it was a thousand times worse for her. But there had to be a way out. A solution that didn't involve Gordy getting arrested, or losing her child, or forgoing the future I had planned with her.

"I don't know what the answer is, but I'm pretty sure there must be one. Promise you won't rush into anything."

"Like what?"

"I don't want to wake up and find a note from you saying you've gone to the police station. If you decide to go there, I'm going with you."

"Why postpone the inevitable? I won't go behind your back, I promise. But I also won't wait much longer."

"Fine. But I need some time to think about this, and I can't do it right now. Things are going to look different in the morning. I feel it."

"I wish I had your optimism. But I don't."

"Then I'll be optimistic enough for both of us."

I said it with a lot more conviction than I felt.

CHAPTER TWENTY-FIVE

I told Gordy I needed to get a good night's sleep so I could figure things out, but every time I closed my eyes, all I could see was her shuffling into a paddy wagon, chains around her ankles, bound for Mexico. I knew it was unrealistic—more likely she'd be shipped off on a plane—but no matter the method of deportation, I couldn't let it happen. I still didn't believe that Gordy was the one who'd run Wynn down. Somebody else had to have driven up that alley after Gordy did. It was the only possible explanation.

I knew Officer Delgado had physical proof that Gordy had driven down that alley, but that didn't mean he had proof that she was the driver who plowed into Wynn. I would bet, though, that once he found the current evidence, he hadn't bothered to look for more. And since he hadn't, that meant I needed to.

It was still dark when I pulled my clothes on and slipped out the door, leaving a note for Gordy. As I drove over to Wynn's house, I visualized finding a large silver bumper that somehow everyone else had missed. I pictured myself parking and walking down the alley, then remembered it was still blocked off. The only way I could access it was through Wynn's backyard, which meant going into her house. I still had the keys, but the moment I used them Queen and Latifah would start barking and wake up Tina who would want to know why I was there. I didn't know what I could tell her. If I said I thought that more than one driver had driven down the alley that night, she'd wonder why I was so concerned about finding another one. She might even cop to the idea that I knew who the current suspect was.

I parked the pickup a couple of doors down from the house and sat in the cab, rubbing my arms to get warm and trying to figure out what to do. It occurred to me that maybe once Officer Delgado had found his evidence, he'd taken the tape away. I got out and walked down the street. The tape was still there.

"Hey!" A voice called out. I spun around. It was Wynn's neighbor, a shy fellow I'd met at her house once or twice although he usually scuttled away when he saw me. His house was behind Wynn's on the opposite side of the back alley. "I know you. You're a friend of Wynn's aren't you?"

"I—yes, yes, I am."

"Terrible, what happened to her."

"Yes."

"I helped 'em catch the guy."

"You did?" I meant to put the emphasis on the word did, but somehow it squeaked out on the word you instead, as if I thought he couldn't possibly have been of assistance.

"Yeah. Found a piece of a vehicle. Handed it over to the officer. He said he'd be able to track down the asshole who drove away."

"You got into the alley from your yard?"

"Uh-huh."

"Will you show me where you found it?"

He cocked his head to one side, a questioning frown on his face.

"Why?"

"Wynn asked me to help the investigation along. She said I could get into the alley from her house, but I don't want to wake Tina up."

"But if I gave them that vehicle part, we don't need to look for anything else."

"Still . . . better safe than sorry. Maybe it won't match anything."

"I guess you're right." He looked miffed, but he gestured with his head that I should follow him into his house. I wondered if the inside of his home matched his yard, which was a colorful mix of native plants and eclectic objects like a stone mermaid whose fluke was missing and a rusty boat propeller. He opened the door and took me through his living room toward the back patio. It was shockingly bare. A sofa and TV were the only furniture in the spacious living room and there were no adornments anywhere. No pictures on the wall, no photographs or bric-a-brac on any shelves. I tried not to stare, but he must have caught the expression on my face.

"I don't like distractions," he said. "Everything triggers me." He didn't elaborate, but I knew he was a Vietnam vet so I assumed he was talking PTSD. He walked through the patio and toward a gate, pushing away a low-lying branch of the large mango tree that took center stage in his yard. "I planted all the mango trees in this neighborhood," he said proudly.

He opened the gate to the back alley and walked down it, to the part of the side alley where Wynn had been knocked down. "I restacked the wood," he said, pointing to the neat pile of chopped tree limbs. "City couldn't bring the truck down yesterday to pick 'em up."

It was the first time I'd had the opportunity to see exactly where Wynn had lain. The garbage can was still where she'd placed it, beyond the pile of wood. There were piles of leaves everywhere and the earth was dry—we hadn't had rain for weeks.

"Do you think it's possible more than one vehicle came down this alley that night?"

Donte looked at me. "Why d'you ask?"

"I may know the suspect, and I'm not convinced they have the right guy." No need for him to know it was a woman.

He shrugged. "Guess it's possible."

"Mind if I poke around?" It was light by now and I couldn't help thinking there could be other vehicle debris under the leaves.

He nodded and walked away. I thought about where the garbage can was and went to the area where Wynn must have been when she was knocked over. I knelt down and started rustling through the leaves. A minute later I felt a tap on my shoulder.

"This make it easier?" Donte leaned over and gave me a hand rake.

I smiled and took it from him.

"You better put these on too." He handed me plastic gloves.

I started to sift through the leaves, glad for the gloves when I came across clumps of dried-up dog poop. I didn't know what I was looking for, but when I came across a small piece of gray

149

metal, my heart skipped a beat. Gray? Gordy's car was silver, not gray. Did silver cars have parts of their undercarriage that were gray? It seemed unlikely. I tucked it under my shirt.

Maybe my hunch was right—there really was another car involved. I scrabbled around on my hands and knees as if I were Latifah nosing through everything in my path, but came up with nothing. It was getting light and Tina would be out soon with the dogs. I didn't want to bump into her and explain myself. I also needed to leave so I could make sure I got home before Gordy did anything reckless.

Donte had gone back indoors. I pushed open the gate to his yard and went inside.

"Maybe I'll take another look later," he said as I handed him the rake. "If I find anythin', I'll let the cops know."

"I think they're fixated on what they already have."

"I'll pass it on to Tina, then."

"No," I said quickly. "I mean . . . she's got enough on her plate already. Let me give you my cell phone number."

Donte pulled a scrap of paper out of the back pocket of his jeans and I scratched my number on it.

"Thanks for all your help." I knew better than to give him a hug so put my hand forward to shake his.

He ignored it.

"Anythin' to help Winnie." His voice was gruff, but I knew he meant it.

CHAPTER TWENTY-SIX

When I got home, Gordy was fully dressed.
"I'm going to the police station," she said. "There's no point in delaying it. And the longer I wait, the worse it looks."
"I don't think it was you."
"I know we both wish it weren't, but with everything Tina said it must have been. I drove down that alley. I knocked into what I thought was a pile of wood, and my car was messed up. It's a slam dunk and even though I didn't know I was doing it, I became a hit-and-run driver."
"Yeah, we know you drove down the alley, but what if you weren't the only one? What if someone drove down after you did and that's who smashed into Wynn?"
"But the officer only found proof from my car."
"Maybe because he'd already convinced himself you were the perp. I went over there this morning. And look!" I held out the small piece of gray metal. "I think I may have found a piece from a different vehicle."
For a moment Gordy's eyes lit up like the Gulfport Christmas tree outside the Casino. They quickly clouded over. "It could be anything. And who knows how old it is?"
"It's gray. Wynn said the car was gray or silver, she wasn't sure which. Officer Del latched onto it being silver because he found your car at Rico's. But what if there were another car? A gray one."
Gordy had her small suitcase on the bed and was folding

clothes in it. She shrugged."
	I spun her around to face me. "Give me twenty-four hours. If I can't find anything, we'll go to the police station together. Hang out here today. I have more ideas. You said there was a U-Haul blocking the street you were on, right?" Gordy nodded. "I'm going over to that house. I'll talk to whoever moved in, ask them about other cars that drove down there. Maybe someone got pissed off at them for blocking the road and that's why they backed up and roared down the alley without seeing Wynn."
	"If that's what you think happened, go to the police. Tell them. They're the ones who should be investigating it, and they have a lot more authority than you do to talk to people."
	"I know. But sometimes these things are better done by someone who really cares." I had a sudden image of what had happened at that fast food restaurant just over a year ago. How one person who cared was able to unmask a killer. I was there. I knew what a difference being passionate about an outcome made.
	"Just promise me you won't do anything today. I don't want to find the missing piece of the puzzle and get home to discover you've disappeared or turned yourself in."
	Gordy sighed, a grim ghost of a smile on her lips. "A puzzle piece? This isn't some children's toy, like the 100-piece jigsaws Sammy likes to do. This is a double-sided 10,000-piece puzzle with hidden images and no picture to guide you."
	I stared at her.
	"You're a puzzle addict."
	"How do you know?"
	"Takes one to know one. I should have figured you'd be totally into them. I have a stack in my spare room, though I admit the largest is only 2,000 pieces and it's only one-sided. Still, that should keep you busy for the day."
	"You really think I'm going to sit here and lose myself in a puzzle?" She picked up the small framed photo of Sammy she'd put on the bedside the night before and placed it on top of her clothes.
	I ignored her pessimism, took the photograph out of her suitcase and placed it back on the nightstand. I took her hands in mine and looked into her eyes. "It's exactly what you're going to do. For him and for me, if not for yourself. Promise you'll be here when I come back."

She stared into my eyes. I could see she was wavering.

I glanced at the piece of gray metal. "I'm going to prove your innocence. I believe in you, even if you don't."

She closed her eyes and when she opened them, I could see she was blinking back tears. She nodded her head, her dark curls falling over her forehead.

"Twenty-four hours. I can't wait any longer."

§

I drove back to Wynn's neighborhood. When I got there, I realized I didn't know which house it was the people had been moving into. I tried to remember if Wynn had mentioned any of her neighbors moving out, but before the accident we mostly discussed our businesses or our personal lives. I'd met a couple of her immediate neighbors and knew she was good friends with them. But I didn't know about the rest of the block.

A loud noise was coming from the end of the block. Sounded like they were having a party, even though it was the middle of the day. Loud rock music blared and voices yelled. That was when I remembered that Wynn had mentioned there was a house down the street that was trouble. It had come up when I discussed possible locations for Kit-Kat's.

"Just be careful," she'd said. "Even the best neighborhoods can have a trouble spot or two. Down the street from me there's a bungalow that has different renters every month. I think it's some sort of halfway house, but not the kind that has someone in charge who helps the residents. This one, the people pay rent, share rooms and never last very long. You never see them move in or out. I don't think they have any belongings. They're probably straight out of the hospital or jail, and as long as the landlord gets paid up front he could care less what they do. The cops are always being called out there because someone overdosed or passed out. Val told me she's asked the police why they can't do something about the owner, but apparently everything he does is legal. So make sure you check all the houses and businesses wherever you plan on locating your cafe."

Surely at a house like that somebody would have heard something. I walked toward the noise.

A middle-aged man and woman were sitting on rickety-looking rattan chairs, half-empty bottles of beer on the table in front of them. A stained mattress was on the front curb waiting for pickup and the yard was littered with empty cigarette packets. A tattered Grateful Dead T-shirt barely covered the large belly of the guy, while the skinny woman next to him was swamped in an outsize Hello Kitty nightshirt. They called out as I approached.

"Hi there. Wanna join us?"

I didn't, but then again, it could be a good idea. "Sure," I said and sauntered over. They looked surprised. I guessed they called out to everyone as a way to preempt any kind of judgmental comments by passers-by. My choice of seating was a filthy rocking chair or a dirty white plastic chair. I chose the plastic.

"You like this neighborhood?" I asked.

"Why? You thinkin' of movin' here?"

"Maybe. Friend of mine lives down the street."

"Which one's that then?" The woman took a slug of beer as she spoke.

"Her name's Wynn. She has a couple of dogs and a couple of daughters who went to college recently."

"Don't know her. Neighbors here aren't too friendly."

I had a feeling I knew why. "Lived here long?" I asked.

"'Bout a month."

"So you must've been here when she got knocked down in a hit-and-run a few nights ago."

"Is that why the police were pokin' around the other day?" asked the Deadhead. "We didn't answer the door when that cop knocked. Don't need no trouble from no one."

"He probably wanted to know whether you saw or heard anything." I paused and tried to make my voice casual. "Did you?"

They shook their heads. I realized that if they were drinking at this time of day, they'd probably both been passed out drunk by that time in the evening.

"We haven't even offered you anything," the woman said, making no attempt to get up. The man frowned at her.

"That's okay. I need to get going anyway." I stood up. "Nice talking to you. Have a good day."

"You should move onto this street." The man said. "You're the first one who's been friendly to us."

I'd been about to walk away, but now I turned back toward

them. "Talking of moving, I heard someone moved in the day my friend was knocked down. Do you know who that would have been?"

The woman pointed across the street to a purple bungalow with sage green trim. "That'd be the faggots over there. This whole town is overrun with queers."

My stomach clenched and my fists along with it. I willed myself to keep my hands to myself, then forced a smile on my face. "Well, now we know why nobody talks to you," I said. "It's not because you drink, or because you leave trash in your front yard. It's because you're bigots. We don't tolerate that in this town. Take it from this Jewish dyke," I said as I stomped away, dusting dirt off my shorts.

CHAPTER TWENTY-SEVEN

Unlike the bungalow I'd just left, this one was immaculate. A neat line of spider plants lined the walkway up to the front door, which looked freshly painted. I rang the bell and waited. There was no reply. Hardly surprising really. It was already mid-morning and most people would be at work. I'd have to come back in the evening.

I wondered who else I could talk to, then realized I probably ought to go visit Wynn. She and Tina both knew my schedule and they'd be surprised if I didn't visit. If Gordy hadn't come to stay, I certainly would have already made my way over there. I had to keep remembering that from Wynn's perspective I knew nothing about the driver who'd put her in this horrible situation. I jumped into the truck, and within half an hour I was sitting at Wynn's bedside.

Her arms were no longer in the contraption they'd been in. Both had casts on them, but not the entire length of her arms.

"They operated on them both yesterday," she said. "I'm on the mend."

"That's great."

"And they're satisfied there's no internal bleeding from my spleen, so if all goes well, I get to go home in a couple of days."

"That's fantastic."

"Yeah." She smiled, a mischievous twinkle in her eye. "Tina enjoyed last night. Know what she calls your girlfriend?"

I shook my head.

"Gorgeous Gordy. She said she's amazing looking."

"She is." I said. Gordy was the last person I wanted to talk about right now. "Have you heard any more from Officer Del?" I tried to keep any trace of anxiety out of my voice.

Her face fell a little. "Only that there's still no sign of the woman who did it. But I don't get it. If she didn't know she did it, why would she have run when Del talked to her? I mean, why not just explain that she had no idea she hit me?"

"Maybe she had no car insurance."

"They checked. She did. Although I will tell you one thing. They said her driver's license lists a different address than where she's living. So there's obviously something suspicious going on."

"Maybe she just never got around to updating her address with the DMV."

"I don't know. Del was going to check it out."

"Last time I saw you, you were worried he wasn't doing enough. Are you sure he has the right person?" I asked.

"Of course. He said she pretty much admitted it was her."

"But how could she have admitted it, if she didn't know she did it?"

"I don't know. But he found her SUV, so he doesn't even need her to admit it."

"A silver one, right?"

Wynn nodded.

"Didn't you tell me originally you thought it was gray?"

"Silver, gray, it's all the same isn't it?"

I shook my head. "Not really. Silver and gray are pretty different."

Wynn looked at me quizzically. "What's going on, Kat? Have you heard something about Officer Del? Is he crooked or something?"

"No. At least, not as far as I know. I'm sure he's doing a good job. I just wondered, if maybe he wasn't being thorough enough. Maybe he should have talked to more people, done a better search in the alley."

"But why would he need to if he already found the vehicle and the driver?"

I sighed.

"So you're going home soon. Are you going to let Tina stay

home and take care of you?"

"I don't think I have a choice. It breaks my heart, but what else can I do?"

§

I left the hospital wondering what my next step was. Gordy would go to the cops tomorrow if I didn't find something today. I decided to talk to Suzie, my car mechanic. Maybe she'd have some ideas.

"So you're saying the suspect—who you currently refuse to name—admits she drove into a pile of wood, but you don't think she drove into Wynn." Suzie said, after I'd explained everything to her as vaguely as I could.

I nodded. We were sitting in the tiny, cramped office she used for doing paperwork. Suzie and Shay had bought the auto mechanic's business several years ago. They'd been so excited to have the opportunity that it was only after they'd started running it that they discovered how much they'd overpaid. The man they purchased it from had given them a long list of customers and assured them the business was flourishing. He failed to mention that he'd been losing customers steadily for years, which was why he was selling. If they hadn't been new to town the couple would have known what a horrible reputation the guy had, but they'd been so excited to discover a business available in the little town they'd decided to make their home that they hadn't done due diligence. As a result it was only now, five years later, that they were finally turning a profit. But the stress had taken its toll and even though they were still joint owners, they'd split up two years earlier.

"Did the cop tell you what kind of damage the vehicle sustained? Damage to the vehicle hitting a woodpile would probably be the front quarter panel, marker lights, headlights, hood, and grill and bumper on that side. There might also be damage to the radiator, water pump and pulley. Even the front strut system. If there were a second vehicle that hit your friend but not the woodpile, the damage would probably be similar but not as severe. A person is soft body mass, but the woodpile would have provided a solid hit. The second vehicle damage would probably be a large dent in the hood, and one of the headlight assemblies might be partially broken."

"So you're saying if the suspect's vehicle sustained all the damage you described to the first vehicle, then likely it didn't hit Wynn, just the woodpile?"

I couldn't believe it! Maybe I'd just found the answer to all our problems.

"We-ll, not necessarily. If Wynn was pushed into the woodpile by the suspect's vehicle, then we could be looking at similar damage as the first vehicle."

"Oh." I felt as if I were on one of those state fair roller coasters I would never choose to ride in a million years. One moment I was at the top of the ride, and a moment later I'd plunged to the depths.

"But I still think it wouldn't have been as severe. Maybe the front corner panel, headlight and marker light assembly damage, even a smashed grill and maybe a slight bumper damage being pushed in. But I think the bumper on the first vehicle would be much more dented. When did you say all of this happened?"

"A few days ago. Why? Did the police come to your shop? Do you have a vehicle that might match what we're looking for?"

"They didn't come. Which is a bit surprising if they were checking all the body shops in the area. But no, I wouldn't have been able to help them. I haven't had any vehicles with those kinds of issues in the last week or so. But—" Suzie leaned toward me and I wondered what she was going to say. "You know all those kids who go to a drugstore and ask for condoms for 'my friend'?" She made air quotes around the words. "Is it you? Are you involved in this? Because if you are, I want to be there for you." She clasped my hands in hers. "Let me help you, Kat."

I pulled my hands away. "It's not me," I said. "Honestly."

"Uh-huh." Her tone made it sound like she didn't believe me for a minute. "I have friends in all the right places. This doesn't have to be as bad as you might think."

If only she were right. But the clock was ticking and even though she hadn't given me all the answers, she'd given me a lot to think about. I needed to go back and see if the U-Haul people were home. But before that I had some questions for Gordy.

CHAPTER TWENTY-EIGHT

Despite her misgivings, Gordy clearly hadn't been able to help herself from becoming completely absorbed by the jigsaw puzzle. The edge was done and she'd sorted a few of the pieces into groupings, while completing small parts of the puzzle randomly. Exactly the way I would have done it. I knew people who would sort through an entire puzzle before they began working on it, putting the pieces into color groupings, but that, to me, was the ultimate in boring. I shouldn't have been surprised that without knowing it, she'd chosen my favorite jigsaw puzzle. I only did most puzzles once, then passed them on. But every now and again there was one I couldn't wait to start almost as soon as I'd finished it and taken it apart.

"I don't get it," Cindy used to say when we were together. "What's the point of spending all those hours putting it together if you just break it up a day later?"

The thing about jigsaw puzzles is, you either get it or you don't. Cindy didn't. But Gordy most certainly did. An ideal puzzle was one that was challenging but not impossible. One where you used skill and attention to tiny details to find the exact right piece, not one of those European castles where one quarter of the pieces were gray stone and another quarter were an endless blue sky with no clouds and no variations in color, so that you had to keep on trying every piece before slotting in the correct one. Gordy had chosen the 2,000-piece Spanish flamenco dancers who, to a novice, might look indistinguishable with their flowing black hair, their flounced dresses, their arms and hands undulating with wooden castanets. In actuality they all had unique characteristics. The scarlet ruffles with white polka dots were quite different from the scarlet ruffles with black dots, and the light wood castanets were emblazoned with completely different designs than the slightly darker wood ones.

She looked up sheepishly when I came in.

"Glad to see you're still here," I said, going over and rubbing her shoulder.

"I said I would be. Despite my craziness yesterday, I really do keep to my word."

"Have you eaten?" I asked, knowing full well what the answer would be. Judging by the progress she'd made on the puzzle, I doubted she'd moved from the table even to pee.

She shook her head. "Although now that you mention it, I could do with something to eat and drink." She stood up and headed for the bathroom. When she returned, she asked, "Did you get what you were looking for?"

"I think I may be making progress. Tell me about the damage to your Hyundai."

"I told you. The front was bashed in."

"I know that, but tell me what you mean by the front. The bumper? The grille? How about the headlights?"

"Honestly, I didn't pay that much attention. When it happened, I was too freaked out about being late to Dana's to see exactly what the damage was. Then I was busy putting Sammy to bed and thinking about you. I know the bumper was hanging loose because I remember it scraping the ground on my way to Rico's. But once I gave it to him and he said he'd take care of everything, I just let him."

"Then I probably need to talk to him. Can I do that?"

"Sure. But I don't see why that will help."

"Because I'm thinking that maybe your vehicle sustained more damage than it should have if all you did was knock Wynn down."

"All I did? Isn't that enough? Dios mio, she's your friend. How can you say that?"

"I know she was hurt and hurt badly. But I'm just not convinced you're the one who did it. Did Rico give you a copy of the work order?"

"He may have. I don't remember. I think he said something about giving me an itemized receipt with all the parts he replaced. Honestly, I don't know. I was in too much of a hurry to flee, and I trust him. I just gave him the money and ran."

"I'm sure he would have given you some paperwork. If you want to sell the car in the future, you'll need to know what things you've had replaced. Especially if it was in an accident. Didn't he hand you any documentation when you gave him the money?"

She screwed up her eyes and I was reminded of an item I'd seen on TV recently about why people close their eyes when they're trying to remember things. Though I was damned if I could remember what the reason was.

"Maybe . . . maybe he said something about leaving the paperwork under the dashboard? With the registration, perhaps. I'll go see."

She returned from the garage a few minutes later, waving papers at me. "I guess he did give me the work order as well as an itemized receipt."

I looked through it quickly. Suzie had been good. She'd got it almost detail for detail. The front bumper, the headlights, the grille. I wondered how Rico had managed to replace everything so quickly. He must have really had to run around to get all the parts. It said a lot about how high his esteem was for his cousin. But it also said something about the shoddy police work of Officer Del. Hadn't he noticed that was an awful lot of damage for a moving body to make to a vehicle? I remembered what Suzie had said about the damage inflicted if the driver had pushed Wynn into the woodpile, which clearly they had, given all her injuries. My mechanic still didn't think it would have been as bad as this list portrayed.

Which meant my instincts were right. Gordy wasn't the driver. But if Gordy wasn't the driver, who was? And how could I possibly find out in time to stop her from turning herself in at the police station?

CHAPTER TWENTY-NINE

My next stop was to visit the couple who'd left their U-Haul in the middle of the street that night. I already had intense feelings of dislike for them, knowing that if only they'd moved their damned truck, none of this would have happened.

Two men were in the front yard, both holding small cans of turquoise paint, which they were applying to the window frames. They put the cans down when I walked up the flagstone path and introduced themselves as Norm and Larry. In my anxious state, I forgot instantly who was who.

"That day was so crazy," said the short one. "We drove all the way from Washington in one day. I said all along that we should break the drive into two and stay somewhere around Savannah, but Norm insisted we didn't need an overnight." So the short one was Larry. He glared up at his partner, a thin lanky man who looked as if he constantly had to stoop if he wanted to have any hope of making eye contact with anyone.

"We left at four in the morning," said Norm. "We should have easily arrived in Gulfport by five or six o'clock that evening. But traffic around Orlando was awful. We were held up for hours."

"I told him not to take I-4. Everyone we know said to take I-10 over to 301 South but he insisted on following the GPS."

"What's the point of having one, if you don't follow it?" said Norm, looking down at me, as if waiting for me to concur. I didn't care which route they took, but I needed to appear interested, so I plastered a smile on my face and intimated that he should continue.

"When we got to Jacksonville, GPS lady said we were only four hours away and that it was 20 minutes quicker to take I-95 to I-4. We would have been fine if there hadn't been a security scare at Disney World." He stooped in my direction and said, "Just my luck. They closed the whole freeway down when we were half an hour outside Orlando. I mean, when does that ever happen?"

"Never," said Larry. "But Jason and Jonathon told us not to come that way. If it hadn't been that, it would have been something else."

The news had been full of the terrorist threat at Disney. Even though it had turned out to be a false alarm, tourism was the lifeblood of this area. If tourists were deterred from coming to Orlando, Tampa Bay would be affected too. But I had my own concerns right now, and they had nothing to do with Mickey Mouse and tourists. I wondered how I was ever going to get a word in edgewise. Norm was gearing up to answer, but I decided it was time to cut in.

"So, you got here at 9.30 p.m. and started unloading your U-Haul."

"We didn't want to leave all our valuables in the truck for someone to steal. Did we break a rule? Is there some neighborhood association we didn't know about? We don't normally do anything like this. I hope we didn't make too much noise. If we did, we'll go to every one of our neighbors and apologize. But so far nobody's complained directly to us, so we had no idea—"

"No," I said, "that's not why I'm here. You must have heard that there was an accident in the alley down the street that night. A hit-and-run."

"Oh my gosh, no." Norm put his hand over his chest, and his face had an expression of horror. I liked these two men, but did they have any sense of just how stereotypical they were? They were almost like a parody.

"We had no idea," Larry said. "Well, thank goodness we decided to unload the truck." The two men had been squaring off, and I'd wondered how on earth they managed to sustain a relationship with so much bickering, but now it was replaced by a completely unified front. They were staring at each other and with one breath they exclaimed, "The Tiffany lamps!" and then, "Exactly!" I presumed they had some expensive light fixtures that could have been smashed if someone had crashed into their truck.

They were still shuddering when I said, "you didn't witness the accident?"

They shook their heads.

"Did you hear anything? Screeching brakes? Thumps or crashes?"

They looked at each other. "I might have . . ." Norm said.

"I might have too," said Larry.

"When we were setting up the four-poster?" Norm's tone was a question.

"Right!" Larry turned to me. "We didn't unpack the entire truck that night. We were so exhausted. We pulled out all of our most precious stuff and then decided we couldn't do any more. We started putting the bed together so we could make it up and get into it."

I smiled to myself. When Cindy and I had moved, we'd slept on a mattress on the floor for days. Clearly not Larry and Norm's scene.

"When we were screwing the posts together, I remember hearing a noise and saying to Norm that I wondered what it was."

"No," said Larry, "it was when we were putting the sheets on the bed."

Norm paused. "You're right."

"You didn't go outside at the point? You didn't see anything?"

"We did go back outside. In fact, we saw a police cruiser. But we didn't think there'd been an accident. The seller of this house was very candid with us. She told us there was one bad house on the street where police get called all the time, but that it was always an internal problem—fighting between housemates or a suspected overdose. She said none of the residents of that house had ever committed any crimes locally or interfered with any of the neighbors, and when we talked to the young girl next door, she confirmed that. So when we saw the cop car, we assumed they were dealing with someone at the house the seller told us about."

"Who did you say you are again?" Norm asked me. I hadn't. All it had taken was one question and they'd been off and running. This was the first time it had occurred to either one of them to wonder why I was asking these questions. I decided to tell them the truth. Or at least, a close version of it.

"I'm a friend of the woman who got knocked over. She was hurt pretty badly, and she's concerned that the police aren't doing enough to find the driver. They've pinpointed someone, but . . ." I lowered my voice and tried my best to look pitiful. "She's concerned it's not the right guy and that if they don't get the right one soon, it may be too late. All the evidence will be gone."

"Oh!" Larry put his hands to his face, "don't tell me. Racial profiling. I bet you. The suspect is an African-American male who's probably got a degree in architecture, but they picked him anyway. Am I right?"

It would have been easy to say yes, but it wouldn't be fair. I didn't want them thinking bad things about our local law enforcement, especially when they were brand-new to Gulfport. Officer Del might not be doing his job as best he could, but I wasn't about to falsely accuse him of something else.

"No. Nothing like that. It's just . . ." I decided to take a chance. After all, they were new to town. They weren't connected to anyone who knew me or my personal life. "I know the person the police suspect, and I don't think they're right."

Larry narrowed his eyes. "I thought you said you were friends with the person who was knocked down, not the person who caused the accident."

"I did. And I am. I'm also friends with the suspect."

"Awkward," said Norm.

"Very," said Larry. "But I still don't understand. Either the person you know drove their car down that alley and caused an accident, or they didn't. How could there be any question about it?"

"The person I know admits driving down the alley and crashing into a pile of wood, but not crashing into my friend. And I believe her. She—"

"Oh, it's a woman." Larry nodded his head up and down, big exaggerated movements. He smiled, knowingly. "She's your lover. Oh honey, you poor thing. You are really stuck in the middle."

Damn. How had he figured that out? Still, it seemed to be getting me more sympathy, so I decided not to deny it.

"Here's the thing. The victim was knocked over in the alley. Gor—my lover admits driving down the alley to avoid your U-Haul. But I think there was a second driver who also drove down that alley because of your truck. And I think that's who knocked down my friend."

"Wishful thinking?" Norm said, raising his eyebrows. "What do the police say?"

"I . . . I haven't gone to them yet with my suspicions."

"Why not?"

"It's a long story that I won't bore you with. It sounds like you can't help anyway. You just heard the one noise and then came out a few minutes later and saw the police car."

They nodded sympathetically and then Norm's eyes suddenly flared.

"You know what? Larry was right. We did hear a noise when we were putting the bed together. But we heard another noise when we were making up the bed. Remember, honey?" Norm turned to Larry. "I asked you if someone was letting off fireworks and you said maybe an electrical transformer had blown?"

"Oh my goodness. You're absolutely right. We had that whole conversation about noise and—"

I cut him off by flinging my arms around him.

Two noises! They'd heard similar sounds twice. It wasn't just my wishful thinking. My instincts were right.

It was time to talk to Officer Del.

CHAPTER THIRTY

I couldn't wait to tell Gordy what I'd found out.

"It all ties together. Too much damage to your vehicle, Larry and Norm saying there were two loud bangs. We'll go to Officer Del first thing tomorrow and tell him everything. He'll realize it wasn't you."

"What if he doesn't listen? As far as he's concerned he's got his guy, or gal. Why mess with a good thing?"

"Because it's the right thing to do, and he seems like a reasonable person. This isn't some big city where people don't know each other. Law enforcement here are big on community policing. They rely on having a good relationship with members of the community. Officer Del's new, and if he's going to be successful in this town he won't want to get on the community's bad side by arresting the wrong person."

"I hope you're right. It seems like a gamble to me, but on the other hand, I said I was going to turn myself in anyway, so I guess I have nothing to lose."

"Are you kidding? If I thought he'd still arrest you, I'd never let you come along with me. I'd go by myself. In fact . . . perhaps that's what I should do anyway. Come on, let's eat before it gets cold."

I'd stopped on my way home for pizza. I pulled paper plates out of the cupboard behind Gordy and opened up the box. The aroma of cheese and garlic hit my nostrils, and suddenly my stomach told me I was starving. I tore open the little packets of parmesan while Gordy attacked the packets of hot peppers.

"I still can't believe you eat like this," she said. "I only let Sammy have pizza as a special treat. I don't want him getting any bad habits."

"I know, I know. I'm the worst when it comes to what I eat. In another twenty years they'll probably tell me I have high cholesterol, high blood pressure and I'll be fifty pounds overweight. But for now, if I don't eat at work, pizza and burgers are my staples." I picked up a slice dripping with cheese, folded it in half and took the biggest bite I could fit in my mouth.

"I called Sammy while you were out," Gordy said, her eyes misting.

"What did you say to him?"

"That his grandmother is feeling much better and that I'll be home soon. Thank goodness for cell phones. Dana had no idea I wasn't calling from Mexico."

"You must be missing him so much."

"I'm used to sharing custody so today I've been telling myself this is just like any other week when he spends three days with Dana. But even on those days when he's with his other mother, I do miss him madly. It's a weird thing—I enjoy having the freedom to live like an adult and not have my whole focus on being a mom, but at the same time I can never stop myself from thinking about him when he's not in my presence. My first thought when you pulled out that pizza was, "don't let Sammy burn his mouth" even though I knew perfectly well he wasn't here."

"Hopefully after tomorrow, this whole nightmare will be over. You'll go over to Dana's and pick him up, and that will be the end of it."

"I hope you're right. I'm not as optimistic as you are. But maybe that's because nothing bad has ever happened to you."

I still hadn't told her about last year. She had no idea how close I'd come to something very bad happening. I should have told her already, but there was a part of me that was a little ashamed of having made such a poor choice.

We ate our pizza in silence. Gordy was preoccupied and I started to wonder whether there was a possibility that she was right. Might Officer Del go ahead and arrest her without listening to me? I thought about what she'd said about her green card and how an arrest could ruin everything. If only the interview weren't coming up in less than two weeks. If she'd already had it, she'd have her ten-year card and nobody would be checking her record. If she weren't having it, for another few months she'd be fine because by then everything would have blown over and she wouldn't even have to mention it at the biometrics appointment. But right now, if she were arrested this week, even if she were released right away, it might still be enough for them to kick her out of the country.

"Why don't I give Officer Del a call and ask him to meet me somewhere?" I said as I placed the leftover pizza slices in a large plastic bag and into the fridge. "That way he doesn't have to know you're here and I can make sure he's not going to do anything stupid."

She didn't even pause. "No. I told you I'm not waiting any longer. He's just going to think worse and worse of me the longer I wait." She came over to me and spun me around. I wanted to argue with her about Officer Del, but her hands started traveling underneath my shirt and I didn't want them to stop.

"I don't think this is going to be our last evening together, but just in case it is, at least for a while, let's make it really memorable," she said, pulling me toward the bedroom.

I couldn't argue with that.

§

Neither of us slept well. Gordy asked me to call Officer Del to let him know we were coming in to see him. While she was in the bathroom, I put in the call.

"Will you be at the department this morning?" I asked him. "I have some stuff I need to tell you."

"Can't it wait? I don't usually come on shift that early."

"I think you're going to want to hear it as soon as possible."

"Ten o'clock. I'll be there."

"Thanks."

I didn't mention that I was coming in with Gordy. Nor did I mention to her that I hadn't told him she'd be with me.

I had a copy of her work order ready to show him, even though I knew he'd seen the vehicle itself. I had the names, addresses and phone numbers of Larry and Norm. And I had a gray piece of metal in my pocket. I was pretty sure we'd be fine. When we pulled up at City Hall, Gordy started shaking.

"We have this," I said, feeling as confident as I sounded.

"You don't understand the pressure," she said. "Citizens never understand."

"This isn't USCIS or ICE. Nobody's taking you anywhere. This is Gulfport police station, a small, friendly place where my friend is the receptionist. Imagine you're just visiting her with me."

"Easy for you to say. To you, it's a small, friendly place. To me, it's terrifying. I don't think I can move."

"Then stay here in the truck while I talk to him."

Ironically, my words had the opposite effect. She pulled at the passenger door and climbed down. "Let's go." Her tone was grim.

I held her hand and we walked inside.

"Kat!" Carrie Ann saw me as soon as I walked in. "To what do we owe the honor this time? Unpaid bills? Or are you still trying to help your friend Wynn." She stopped talking long enough to notice I wasn't alone. "Oh, is this . . . ?"

"My girlfriend. I'll do the introductions another time. Can you tell Officer Del we're here to see him?"

She nodded. "Then it is that Wynn business. I sure hope they catch the bastard soon."

I felt Gordy's hand go limp, and I gripped it tighter.

A moment later, Officer Del was striding toward us. I was slightly in front of Gordy, and at first he didn't notice her.

"So, what's so urgent it couldn't wait? My wife was—Oh!" Gordy had moved out from behind me. He came toward us. "Gabriella Luna, you're under—"

"No! Don't do that." I said. "You have to listen to what I have to say first. She's innocent."

"I'm sorry to inform you I don't have to listen to what you or anyone else has to say. Please move aside."

"We're here of our own accord. We're not going anywhere. So can we please go into your office and talk? I think once you hear what I have to say, you're going to change your mind."

He hesitated.

"Kat didn't want me to come here," Gordy said. "I was the one who insisted. So don't worry. I'm not going to run away."

"You already did that once." His tone wasn't friendly, but he also hadn't moved any closer to us.

"May we come through?" I used my politest tone.

He nodded. We followed him through the swinging doors and into an interview room.

CHAPTER THIRTY-ONE

Now that we were here, I didn't know how to open the conversation. I was aware that if I made it sound as if I were criticizing Officer Del's detective work, he'd get defensive. I should have planned what to say so that he wouldn't take any of it personally, but I hadn't. Now I couldn't think how to get started. We sat at a square table, Gordy and Officer Del facing each other with me sandwiched in-between.

While I thought what to say, Officer Del jumped in.

"I went to see your friend Wynn yesterday. Showed her some images of vehicles. Guess which one she picked out as the one that hit her?" He waited for one of us to respond, and when neither of us did he carried on. "A Silver Hyundai Tucson. Isn't that the model you drive, Ms. Luna?"

Gordy nodded.

I jumped in. "Did you also show her other vehicles similar to that? Wynn's pretty clueless when it comes to cars. She wouldn't know the difference between a Hyundai Tucson, a Honda CR-V or any other SUV." For someone who didn't want to criticize his police work, I couldn't believe I'd done just that.

"How I do my work is none of your business, Ms. Ayalon. Unless you have some sort of material evidence, then I believe I need to ask you to be silent while I question Ms. Luna. You're lucky I'm even allowing you in the room."

"I'm sorry," I said. "But I do have evidence. I rummaged in my backpack and pulled out the work order. "I'd like you to take a close look at this. It's all the work that was done on Gor—Gabriella's vehicle after the accident." I handed it to him and continued my speech. "Gabriella doesn't dispute she drove down the alley by Wynn's house and damaged her vehicle when she smashed into the pile of branches Donte had piled up by Wynn's garage. But that's exactly the point. She did drive into the woodpile and this proves it. The damage to her vehicle was extensive. If she'd hit Wynn, the damage would have been different, wouldn't it? Hitting a person is very different from hitting a pile of wood."

"That's your evidence?" Officer Del had been scanning the document I'd handed him, but now he slapped it on the table. "She did both—hit Wynn and the wood and that's why she had all that damage."

"There's more. I'm sure you've talked with many of the neighbors, but there are a couple who just moved in. I don't think you found them at home," I said, trying not to add, *if you even went there*. "They're the ones who were moving the night she had the accident. They said they didn't even know about the hit-and-run. But what they did tell me is that they heard not just one bang, but two. When I suggested that they heard Gabriella the first time and some other driver the second time, they thought it was absolutely plausible."

Officer Del sighed. "Are you done?"

I decided to play my trump card. I pulled out the gray piece of metal I'd found in the alley. "I know you searched the alley and found pieces of Gabriella's vehicle. But when I looked, I also found this." I thrust the metal toward him.

"So you went into the crime scene despite the tape that was across it?"

Shit. I forced myself to think quickly, not my strong suit. "I—I was walking the dogs. Wynn's dogs. One of them broke loose from the leash so I had to run after him. I guess he must have been scrabbling in the dirt and that's how come he dug this up."

"So the dog dug up a piece of gray metal and that makes you think what? That the vehicle that hit Wynn was a gray one, not Gabriella's silver Hyundai."

"Exactly!" I let out a deep breath. I hadn't realized until then that I'd been holding it.

"Okay, Ms. Ayalon, now let me tell you something." I didn't like his tone, but perhaps he was just being officious. "First of all, if the dog was scrabbling in the dirt and found something that was buried, then it could have been there for weeks or months. Secondly, you've been talking to people and you think you have all the answers. Well, I've been talking to people as well. After I visited your friend Wynn, I went to see an old friend of Gabriella's. More than a friend, actually. Gabriella's wife." I looked across at Gordy and saw she'd turned pale. He waited, letting the words sink in. I realized he was hoping to catch me off-guard, that he thought perhaps I didn't know she was married.

When I didn't say anything, he turned to Gordy. "You don't dispute that Dana Ashton is your wife."

She shook her head.

"Your wife told me you'd gone to Mexico on a family emergency. Why would she think that?"

"I was going to go." Gordy said.

"After I specifically asked you not to leave town, you were about to flee?"

"It was stupid. I got scared."

"But why would you flee if you were innocent?"

Gordy sighed, but she said nothing.

"I also want to know why your wife said that you live with her at 2014 Jacaranda Drive, Kenwood. And yet your cousin gave me a completely different address for you. The one I found you living in." Gordy sat still, looking down at her hands, which were twitching in her lap.

"So which one is it? Do you live in Kenwood or in Gulfport?"

"I live with my wife, but I'm house-sitting for a friend."

"House-sitting." He repeated the word, but inflected a note of incredulity in it.

She nodded.

"You looked pretty settled to me. No suitcases anywhere in sight. A playroom set up for your son's toys. And perhaps most telling of all—when I excused myself to use the bathroom in the Kenwood house it was pretty clear there was only one adult toothbrush in it. I would never question your son without your permission, but when he saw me there he said, "You're the one who visited my other mommy in my other house." Now why would he have said that if you're just—" he paused to put all the sarcastic emphasis he could on the word—"house-sitting."

"Fine," Gordy snapped. "We're separated."

"Yes. I figured you were. I was just wondering how many more lies you were planning on telling me. Along with the one about you not being the person who smashed into Ms. Ayalon's *dear* friend, Wynn Larimer, four nights ago."

The room was quiet, except for Officer Del drumming his fingertips on the table. He was leaning back slightly, as if he'd set a trap and was just waiting for Gordy to walk into it. I couldn't understand why. All along he'd seemed like a perfectly reasonable man. Why wouldn't he listen to us, and why was he making it all so difficult?

"Please—" I said, but he put his hand up in a stop sign.

"This isn't about you, Kat. This is about Gabriella telling the truth. You can tell the District Attorney and your lawyer and anyone else you choose all your theories about what did or didn't happen. But I'm wrapping up this case. I'm willing to accept that maybe Gabriella didn't know she knocked Wynn down when it first happened. But what I will not accept is that she fled the scene. A hit-and-run that causes serious injuries is a felony offense, and for that there is no excuse. Especially when the perpetrator flees not just once, but twice."

"But—" I tried again, but he put his hand up to halt me.

"You should count yourself lucky I haven't asked you how you knew where Gabriella was. If I thought you'd known ever since she went missing, you might be in serious trouble. So you better think very carefully before you say anything else."

"Are you accusing me—?" I was about to come up with something, but Gordy stopped me.

"Enough!" She leaned in and faced Officer Del square on. "You're right, Officer Delgado. After I drove into that woodpile I should have taken more time to see exactly what happened. I was in a hurry. My wife was mad at me and my child was waiting for me. I didn't look carefully enough. And then when I read about the hit-and-run in the *Gazette*, I freaked out and decided to run. But I'm not running anymore. I'll pay whatever consequences I have to."

Officer Delgado stood up. "In that case, Gabriella Luna, you are under arrest for leaving the scene of an accident that you caused on the night of February first in which you caused serious bodily injuries to Wynn Larimer. You have the right to remain silent . . ." He droned on some more, but all I could think was *this is all my fault.* I had told Gordy to come with me to this interview. I assured her it would all be okay. We'd avoided talking about the elephant in the room—the real reason Gordy was still giving her legal address in Kenwood—but once she was in police custody it was only a matter of time before they looked up her citizenship status. And when that happened, I couldn't bear to think about the consequences.

We'd tried to do the right thing. It had turned out to be wrong. It was up to me to make it right.

CHAPTER THIRTY-TWO

I couldn't miss another day at work. It wasn't fair on Frances. I was already later than usual as I pushed through the staff entrance of the hotel and made my way to the kitchen.

"What the heck, Kat?" Cindy said when she saw my face. I'd sobbed when they took Gordy away, tears of rage, frustration, fear and sadness. My eyes felt as red as the raw meat I pound for scaloppini. I grabbed pots and saucepans and all the other utensils I needed, banging them fiercely as I lined them up, and told Cindy everything that had happened.

"I don't know what to do," I wailed, the tears starting all over again. "She looked defiant when he took her into custody, but I know underneath she's scared shitless."

"I don't get it. If she has her green card, and has been here all these years, she's almost a citizen. Surely that makes her safe?"

"You'd think so, wouldn't you? But I've been reading a lot online and you'd be amazed at how complicated all this stuff is. And so much of it is a gray area. In theory, an arrest shouldn't mean anything if she ends up being acquitted, but it's the timing that's off. If she hadn't already been this far along in the process, she could have waited to apply for her green card renewal until this was all over and she'd have been fine. But it's too late to cancel the application at this point. Now she has two choices. Either she misses her appointment at USCIS and they cancel her application—which by default means she's out of compliance since her green card has to be renewed—or while she's out on bail, she goes to get her final fingerprints done. In that case the first thing that will come up is that she's awaiting trial for a felony offense, which is an instant and massive red flag."

Cindy came over and put her arm around me. "Sounds complicated. When might she get out?"

"She has to have a court hearing within twenty-four hours. The arraignment's not for another month or more."

"If you could get more definitive proof it's not her, could you get her released before she goes in front of the judge?"

"I don't know. But it's a moot point. I don't have any other proof."

Cindy turned me sharply to face her. "Then go find some. If she really wasn't the driver—"

"*If* she wasn't the driver? You don't believe me?"

"Sweetie, I have no idea what happened. But if you want to fight for your girl, then you can't sit here and wail to me. If she wasn't the driver, there's another vehicle out there that needed repairs. Go to every frigging auto mechanic in Gulfport, and when you've talked to all of them, start in St. Pete. Someone has to know something."

"I can't. In case you haven't noticed, there's a restaurant lunch that needs preparing. I'm already behind on it."

"I've watched you enough times . . . . I'll get things started. Frances had a new guy, Troy, covering for you yesterday. I know he isn't employed elsewhere, so he should be able to come in again." She pointed to the corkboard where staff left messages for each other. "That's his number pinned up there. Call him!"

Half an hour later, Troy was in the Garrett's kitchen and I was on the phone with Suzie, making sure I knew exactly what questions to ask when I approached the auto mechanics.

"Why don't I come with you?" she said, her voice slightly muffled by heavy machinery in the background. "Things are under control at the shop, and there may be questions I need to ask that you won't think of."

I didn't want to owe her anything, especially as I wasn't entirely sure of her motives, but I wasn't about to pass up anything that could help get Gordy released, so I agreed to it.

We started at the largest place in the area, Corrigan's, on Pasadena. Suzie knew the owner, Jim, a friendly looking guy with large, clean hands despite his oil-stained coverall. Without going into the exact details, she told him what we were looking for.

"I've had a couple of accident-related vehicles this week, but doesn't sound like anything you're looking for. One was a rear-ender. The driver of the other car was texting, didn't notice she was coming up on a traffic light and went straight into my poor guy who was waiting for the red light to change. The other was a woman who misread the signs at that intersection on Pasadena and 66th and had a head-on when she chose the wrong lane to turn onto Pasadena. Good luck to her getting a new insurance policy." He raised his arms up and to the sides in a gesture of emptiness.

"You got any suggestions for us?" Suzie asked. "Especially if it were someone who wasn't being totally honest about what happened."

"You may want to focus on paint jobs. If the driver doesn't want his vehicle to be noticed, the first thing he'd do is get it painted."

"Even before the repair?" I asked.

"Depends on the damage. If the bumper came off, they might spray paint the rest of the car and then order a replacement bumper. But if it had a big dent, they'd probably have to wait until they got the replacement body-part."

"Do you question it if someone comes to you and wants their vehicle spray-painted?"

"It's not up to me to ask why customers want stuff done to their cars. But if it was clear someone had been in an accident and they seemed kinda sleazy, I'd probably tell them I had too much work to do and refer them elsewhere. I don't want trouble."

"Who would you refer them to?" Suzie asked.

"You won't like my answer," Jim said. "I'd send them to Wally over on 49th."

Suzie made a face, like there was a smell of bad sewage in the air. I looked at her.

"I never send anyone there. We had a run-in early on. Ever since then, whenever I get a good mechanic, sooner or later Wally hears about them and poaches them from me. He's a nasty piece of work."

"I know," said Jim. "And I think he's probably got some

questionable ethics. That's why I send the suspicious-looking folks to him. Figure eventually he'll put a foot wrong and get his due."

"Sounds like Wally should be our next stop," I said.

"Yeah, but don't ask him head-on what you asked me. He'll clam up if there's even a hint of what you're looking for. You'll have to figure out a different way to get information from him."

We left Jim and headed over to 49th. "You'll have to handle this one on your own," said Suzie. "As I said, I don't have a good relationship with him."

As we drove over, I formulated a plan in my head. Suzie dropped me a block away and said she'd wait by the supermarket. I crossed the road and walked across the forecourt to the door that had the word "office" above it.

The man behind the counter had jowls a little like Wynn's larger dog, and the bags under his eyes suggested he was either an insomniac or a heavy drinker. A younger man was behind him, sorting through the keys that were hanging on a pegboard to the side. I wished I could have dealt with him instead.

"How can I help you, young lady?" His smile was more like a leer and I disliked him instantly.

"I heard through the grapevine you might be the man I'm looking for." I forced a sickly sweet smile onto my face.

He grinned. "Music to my ears. I'm a married man, but you know how it is . . ." He pushed his greasy hands through his hair as if he were Elvis making some sort of sexy move.

"The cops are looking for my car. It's a long story and I could tell it to you if I had the time, but I don't. I heard you might be able to help me disguise it a little, you know, maybe spray paint it or make some changes to it . . ."

His eyes narrowed. "Where is it right now?"

"In my garage at home. I don't want it to be seen."

He shook his head. "Sorry, honey, can't help you. At least not with that. If you're looking for a virile stud that's a different story."

"I'm disappointed. I heard you were the guy."

"Then you heard wrong. Everything I do is strictly above board. Maybe the next guy you go to, you better not tell them the cops are after you."

Damn. "Would that have made a difference?"

He shrugged. "Maybe. Don't ask, don't tell," he said, looking me up and down. "Know what I mean?"

He knew I was a lesbian. Likely he even knew why I was there, or else he thought I was sent by the police or an insurance company. He'd seen right through me.

"Thanks anyway," I said, and pushed through the office door, back onto the forecourt. I trudged across it dejectedly. This was useless.

"Excuse me." I heard a low voice from behind me and turned around. It was the mechanic who'd been in the office. "You forgot this," he said, putting something in my hand, then disappearing as quickly as he'd appeared.

I waited until I'd crossed the road and was back with Suzie to look and see what it was.

A business card for a man named Len Cardoza, Auto Consultant. A handwritten scrawl said, "Tell him Pete sent you."

CHAPTER THIRTY-THREE

"I've never heard of Len Cardoza," Suzie said when she examined the business card. "But Pete used to work for me. He's a good guy. If this is some shady business, I can't believe he's got himself mixed up in it."

There was no phone number on the card but the address was a side-street only a couple of miles away. As we drove over, I tried to make small talk with Suzie.

"You seeing anyone nowadays?" I asked.

"Can't seem to make myself. Guess I'm still not over Shay. Though I gotta be honest. If you were a free woman . . . but I know you're not. And even then I don't know if I could really go through with it."

I ignored the second part of what she said. "Must be hard, working together after you split up."

"I'd never want anyone else as my business partner. But yeah, sometimes I figure I'd get over her quicker if I didn't spend so much time with her. Truth is, there's a part of me hoping we'll still get back together again."

"I heard she was dating someone pretty seriously, that woman, Jen, who runs the big charity in St. Pete?"

"I know." Suzie laughed a wry chuckle. "I'm hopeless. Maybe if they move in together I'll finally accept we're through." She pulled the Highlander up at an expensive-looking two-story house. "This is it."

Unlike most of the houses on the block, which were pale

stucco, this house was made of brick. There were black metal bars on the windows, unusual for this neighborhood and it was surrounded by low-hanging live-oaks draped heavily with Spanish moss. One side of the house had a tower, and I half expected to see Rapunzel leaning out of it. It was impossible to see what lay beyond the trees surrounding the house. The door was dark heavy wood with a small electric buzzer on one side.

Almost as soon as we rang, the door opened. A well-dressed man in pressed chino pants and a crisp white shirt stood in front of us.

"Pete sent us," I said.

The man didn't move. "Who's Pete?"

"Pete Donaldson," said Suzie. "We heard about the great job you did a few days ago on the gray SUV."

"How does Pete know about that?"

OMG! Suzie's opening was masterful, and just like that he'd confirmed all my suspicions. She had taken a massive leap, and we had landed right where we needed to. I owed her big-time. My heart was thumping so hard I didn't know how not to show it.

"He works for Wally," said Suzie. "Must've overheard something. Told us you're the guy people go to if they need to avoid detection."

"I'm gonna talk to Wally. I don't need his big mouth causing trouble. This is a referrals only business."

"Still . . ." I said, "I'm here now. And I can pay."

"I need money up-front."

"Won't be a problem. Can I see samples of your work?" I held my breath.

"How do I know who you are?" he said.

"I'm Kat Ayalon. Head chef at The Garrett. You can Google me. My picture is on the hotel website." He was already tapping keys on his phone, and a moment later my face lit up his screen. "That's me, and I don't want that image replaced with a mug shot. I borrowed my boss's car. I was drunk. Messed it up. She thinks it was stolen last night from the employee parking lot. I'll lose my job and a whole lot more if she finds out the truth." I couldn't believe how smoothly I blended fact and fiction despite my racing pulse and thumping chest.

He frowned, but finally he moved aside and took us down a short hallway into a plain-looking office where two LED screens sat on an empty oak desk. He clicked on the keyboard and both screens lit up.

One side showed a red pickup truck with its flatbed smashed in and taillights hanging down. The other screen depicted a yellow pickup with red and gold flames painted down both sides of the flatbed.

"Before and after," he said. "Satisfied?"

"Amazing!" I breathed. "I think I've seen that pickup around town."

"Sure you have. I make my vehicles stand out on purpose. People who are trying to hide something usually think a neutral color will serve them best. I do the opposite, make the vehicles so outrageous when people see them, they're too busy noticing the design to imagine this is a vehicle they might be on the lookout for."

"The one from the other day started out gray. What color did it end up?" I asked, my fingers metaphorically crossed so hard they hurt.

He clicked an arrow on the keyboard in front of the screens and two images came into view. On one side a gray Nissan Rogue with a massive dent in the side, broken headlights, and various other bits of damage I wasn't skilled enough to identify. On the other, a putrid purple SUV with psychedelic hippie designs on the side and a purple luggage rack fixed on top.

"I haven't seen that one around," said Suzie.

"That's because the owner and I had a . . . dispute about the cost. He only brought me the final payment yesterday so I held onto it until then."

"You do them on site?" Suzie asked. "Your property is big enough that you probably have room out back, right?"

"I don't give my customers any details. The less you know the better."

"That's fine," I said. "Looks like you're discreet, which is what I need. How do I pay you?"

"Cash up-front. Bring $10,000 and after I've seen the extent of the damage I'll let you know how much more I need."

"No problem," I said. "And if you do as good a job on mine as you did on those others, I'm going to treat you to a gourmet five-star meal at our hotel."

"It's a deal," he said, without extending his hand for me to shake.

"There's no phone number on your card. How do I call you?"

"You don't. I don't need anybody taping my phone conversations or making copies of emails to use against me. It's a gentleman's agreement. I know your name and you know mine— or at least the name I've given you. This is my office, not my home. I'm here for two hours a day, from 11.00 a.m. to 1.00 p.m. every day. You have an hour and a half if you want to bring your car in today. Otherwise, you'll need to wait until tomorrow."

CHAPTER THIRTY-FOUR

When we were a block away, I asked Suzie to stop the car. As soon as she put it in park, I flung my arms around her.

"We did it!" I said. "I'll never be able to thank you enough."

"It's not over yet," she said.

"Almost. All I have to do is go to Officer Del . . ."

"Not yet, you don't."

"Why not?"

"He didn't want to listen to you this morning. What makes you think he will now?"

"We'll get him to go back there with us. You heard the guy; he's there for another hour."

"And the moment he sees a cop car he'll wipe that computer clean, head out the back door, and you'll never find him again."

I thought for a moment. I was so close to having everything sorted out, and all I could think of was getting Gordy home. I didn't want her to spend a single night locked up.

"You don't think he's got vehicles he's working on out back, in the yard or in a garage onsite?" I asked.

"Maybe he does and maybe he doesn't. But you can't risk it. He has to be caught red-handed."

"How?"

I twisted around to face her. If she'd been standing, I had the sense she'd have had her hands on her hips and been shaking her head from side to side. As it was, she was looking at me as if I were a little slow.

"You gotta take your truck to him."

"But my truck's in perfect condition."

"Sacrifices, kiddo, sacrifices."

"You mean, I need to bash my truck in on purpose just so I can bring it to him?"

"Unless you know of some other vehicle."

"I don't suppose you've got some clunker in your garage right now . . ."

"Sweetie, I can help you as much as possible. But I can't put my business in jeopardy by bringing a customer's car to this sleaze. This is something you're going to have to do yourself."

"I don't have time."

"Yes you do. I'll drive you home, you get in your truck and go crash it somewhere. Just don't do anything too serious to it."

"And where am I going to get $10,000 in cash? He said I have to bring that before anything else."

"Take the truck over and tell him you need a couple of hours to get the money. Assure him you'll deliver it tomorrow. Meanwhile, he has your truck as collateral."

"I love my truck." I tried not to pout. For the longest time I didn't even own a vehicle. It was easy enough to get around Gulfport without one and I used to bicycle everywhere. But Wynn had said if I were serious about getting my business going, I'd need a pickup. My bronze Ford Ranger was ten years old, but she ran beautifully.

"If you're one of those gals who love your truck more than your woman . . ." There was a glint of humor in her eye, but I couldn't see anything to laugh at. She was right, though.

"Fine. I'll do it. Can you come with me? I've never crashed a vehicle into anything before."

An hour later, my beloved Ranger had a large dent in the flatbed and had been delivered to Len. Suzie's prediction had been right: he agreed to let me deliver the money the next day. As we drove away, I called Officer Del.

"If you're looking for Gabriella, she's up at the county facility. We don't book people here."

"And then will they let her go?"

"I don't know. Someone who flees the scene of a crime in a hit-and-run isn't exactly a good candidate for being relied upon to show up to a court hearing. Especially in a case like this where she avoided arrest once she thought we were looking for her."

"But she turned herself in. And she's got no record. And she's a professional with a job. Doesn't that count?"

"It might. Or they might decide to have her go in front of a judge and let him or her decide."

"Is there any way you can get her released, or postpone her court appearance? And before you think I'm just someone who can't take no for an answer, I have new evidence. Definitive evidence that she wasn't the driver."

I told him what had transpired with Len. To my surprise, he was surprisingly receptive. He wanted to hear more.

"Where are you?" he asked. "I want to talk to you and get all the information you have on this guy."

"I'll come to you," I said and asked Suzie to drop me off at City Hall.

"Let me know how it goes." Suzie gave my arm a squeeze as I climbed out of her SUV a few minutes later.

"Thanks for everything. I owe you big-time."

She shrugged. "An invitation to your wedding will be a good start."

Officer Del was more animated than I'd ever seen him. "There have been a series of crimes committed with vehicles that seem to disappear. We thought they'd been shipped off to Mexico or Guatemala, but maybe they're right here in our backyard after all. This could be really big news. And I'll be the one—" He stopped himself. I knew what he was about to say, though. He'd get credit for finding this guy. So much for teamwork.

"Glad to help. So you'll put in the call or fill out the paperwork, or whatever, to get Gabriella released?"

"I can't do that until I see those images for myself. If they don't release her this afternoon, she may need to stay overnight until she has a hearing tomorrow morning. Don't worry, if she's innocent, we'll drop the charges."

"But why should she spend even one night in jail if she didn't commit a crime?"

"Because that's the way it works. There are people who spend weeks, even months in jail when they're not guilty. People who aren't granted bail, or those who can't come up with bail money, have to sit and wait for their day in court, however long it takes. I had to work hard to justify the arrest. Now that Gabriella's over at County, I have to justify a request to release her. I can't do that on your say-so. But if what you say is true, we'll have her out soon enough."

I groaned.

"It happens all the time," Del said. "It's nothing to worry about. She won't have a record. If anyone's doing a background check, it'll be as if it never happened."

I stared at him. Had police work inured him to people's feelings? I bet he'd feel differently if he'd ever had to spend a day in jail. But even apart from that, there was the whole immigration thing. I glared at him. "You don't understand."

"Actually," he said, returning my glare directly, "I think I do. I know why your friend says she's living with her wife when she's obviously living in Gulfport. It's not that hard to figure out when you consider that Gabriella is from Mexico. I presume she got her green card after they got married. How much longer until she can apply for a green card in her own right?"

I felt my chest start to pound and the blood run to my fists. I was so angry I wanted to hit him. Instead, all the anger and tension, the fear and anxiety I'd felt for the past two days came to a head and I burst into tears.

"You knew?" I could barely get the words out, coughing as I tried to stifle my sobs. "And yet you arrested her for a felony offense, which is a deportable crime? Do you know what kind of trouble she could land in because of you?"

"I'm a peace officer. I do my job. I can't not arrest someone just because of their immigration status. I wouldn't have arrested her if I didn't think she was guilty. But as I told you, once she's out, it will be as if she was never in."

"Easy for you to say. What if she doesn't get out? What if they start deportation proceedings right away?"

"Why would they do that? I mean, yeah, if she's found guilty they could. But not otherwise."

"That's not true. You know Pinellas County cooperates with ICE. When they fingerprint her today, you think they won't start running records and see that she's out of status? Her current green card's already run out."

"Why didn't she apply sooner? Why let herself get out of compliance?"

"She applied as soon as she could. You can only apply to renew the card 90 days ahead. But they never get people scheduled for the renewal in those 90 days. She's luckier than most. Her green card ran out last week and her new biometrics appointment is in two weeks' time."

"So then they'll see that she's got an appointment and she'll be fine."

"It's not that simple. The citizenship and immigration services is a separate agency from ICE. USCIS knows she has an appointment, but they're not law enforcement." I'd spent hours reading up on it, and felt as if I knew more than he did. "I'm begging you, let her out."

He had the decency to look apologetic as he said, "I can't. I'm sorry, but there's no way I can do anything today. I still don't think you have anything to worry about. If ICE is as inefficient as every other government bureaucracy, by the time they realize she's in jail, she won't be anymore."

I could only hope he was right.

I wished there were a way to go back to Len Cardoza's this afternoon, but the guy had made it clear he wouldn't be there. There was nothing to do but wait for a phone call from Gordy. Hopefully she'd be calling for me to pick her up from the county facility. I'd asked Officer Del whether it was worth driving up there, but he said there was no point. I wouldn't be able to see her.

Usually when I'm stressed, I bake. But I didn't want to start something and then get the call so I sat around nervously waiting. As the hours wore on, my hopes for her getting out by the end of the day receded. Finally at 4:00 p.m. my phone rang.

"The court appearance is 8.00 a.m. tomorrow morning." Even though I couldn't see her, I could tell from her voice how despondent she was. She sounded bone tired too.

"I'll be sitting in the front row," I said.

"No point. I won't be there in person. They do it on closed-circuit TV. I'm scared, Kat, really scared."

"Don't be. I have really great news. We found the guy who did it."

"Don't start that again. I'm trying to make peace with my

situation. I keep telling myself that ICE won't find me here, that I'll get out on bail, and that I'll make my appointment at USCIS. I don't need—"

"Listen to me!" I yelled down the phone. "It wasn't you. It definitely wasn't you. I know it and now Officer Del knows it."

I heard a gasp covered by a cough. "What are you talking about? If he thinks I didn't do it, why am I here?"

"It's a long story. If everything goes well, we'll have you out tomorrow. Officer Del assured me that your arrest and any charges they made will be wiped off your record. It'll be completely clean for Immigration."

There was silence on the other end of the line.

"Don't get my hopes up," she whispered, "unless you're absolutely sure."

"Hang in there, my sweetheart, just hang in there."

CHAPTER THIRTY-FIVE

Officer Del agreed to come with me to Len Cardoza the next day, incognito. We met a couple of blocks away. Out of uniform the guy was good-looking if you looked beyond the weird outfit he'd assembled. His eyes were covered with Ray-Bans so dark I wondered how he could see through them. A floral Hawaiian print shirt hung loosely from his shoulders while his butt was encased in tight black pants. I'm no fashionista, but I hoped for his sake that this was something he'd picked specifically for his role today and not his usual casual attire.

We walked together down the street. As we approached the house, he said, "I should have known it would be this one."

I cocked my head to one side.

"The Gothic house, all the trees surrounding it. A yard you can't see from the street—kinda stereotypical don't you think?"

"No more so than your outfit," I snapped.

It was eleven o'clock and Cardoza answered the door the moment I knocked.

"Who's this?" He said when he saw Del. His eyes narrowed. "Why is he here?"

"His name is Roddy, and he's the one supplying me with the cash. Said he wouldn't give it to me unless I could prove what it's for."

Len looked Del up and down.

"Why do you care what she's using it for? You her Daddy?"

Del shook his head but didn't remove his sunglasses.

"What's your relationship then?" Len hadn't budged from the front door.

"I give people loans," said Del.

"Roddy who gives people loans. I've never seen or heard of you before, and I know a lot of people." He turned to me. "I told you to bring the money. I never said anyone else could be with you. I don't like the smell of this."

"He wants to see the kind of work you do." I said. "Then he'll give you the money."

Len's eyes narrowed. "You may trust him, but I don't. I don't know where you found him, but he's no loan shark. And I don't think he's your boyfriend either."

"You said you want the money. I have it. He just wants proof that you're going to take care of my truck."

Len shook his head slowly from side to side. "Our deal is off."

I felt my chest constrict. All I could think of was Gordy. I couldn't fail her now. "We had an agreement. I gave you my truck. You can't just refuse me now."

"Actually I can. I'll get your truck back to you." He started to turn away from us, ready to close the door.

"No!" I shoved my foot in the door jamb, then turned sideways and pushed him out of the way with my shoulder. He was taller and broader than me, but he hadn't been expecting the move and was caught off-guard. He stumbled, and by the time he'd uprighted himself, I was through the door and down the hall. I ran straight into the office and grabbed his laptop.

"What the hell do you think you're doing!" He came at me, but Del had come in after us and grabbed his arm.

"What the—?" He turned toward Del. "You're a cop, aren't you? Don't deny it. I knew it the moment I saw you on my doorstep."

"In that case you'll have no problem with me searching your property."

"You bet I have a problem. No search warrant, no search."

Del dropped Len's arm. Len came toward me and tried to grab the laptop, but I held it close to my chest. I had an awful feeling I'd blown everything. Del couldn't search the property, which meant he probably wasn't entitled to look at the images on the laptop, even assuming there was no password and I could figure out how to bring them up on the screen. But if we left now, Len could wipe the drive clean and get out of Dodge. We didn't even know his real name.

"The SUV you painted purple," I said. "The one from the hit-and-run, that used to be gray. Where does he live?"

"I have no idea what you're talking about."

"You showed me the picture yesterday. I don't care about your business. I just need to find the guy who owns the Nissan Rogue."

Len raised his eyebrows and shrugged. "Still have no idea," he said.

I thought about what Del had told me. That there was a ring of criminals using cars for crimes. Len was surely just one small piece of it.

"You delayed returning the car to him. You said you argued about the cost. But maybe what actually happened was that you found stolen property in the vehicle and asked for a cut. Right?"

Len placed his hands on his hips. "That's enough. You need to put my laptop down," he said to me. "And you both need to get the hell out of my house."

I looked at Del. I was trying really hard not to cry. I'd wanted to help Gordy, yet all I'd done was ruin everything. The moment we left, Len would call the purple Nissan Rogue owner, and the guy would probably spray-paint it himself, a nice soothing tan color or some other bland shade that would make it indistinguishable from all the other SUVs in the area. Assuming he even chose to stay here.

"I just want to help my girlfriend," I said. "She's been arrested for a crime she didn't commit. It was committed by Mr. Purple, the guy you don't like. I know he did something you don't approve of." Len looked taken aback, as if that was exactly what had happened, and I had a sudden moment of complete clarity. "He couldn't stop when he hit Wynn because he was fleeing the scene of another crime! If he'd stopped to help Wynn, what would they have found? Did he kidnap someone? Was there blood in the car? Or stolen goods?"

"That's exactly what happened," said Del, "isn't it?" I swung around and looked at him. He was talking to Len. "You found the silver mermaid in his vehicle, or some evidence that he was the thief." Del turned to me. "She was stolen the same night as that hit-and-run."

I'd read about it in the *Gazette*. A city matriarch, celebrating her ninetieth birthday by opening up her home, robbed of one of her most meaningful possessions.

Now Del spoke to Len. "If you give me that guy, we'll leave your property right now, no questions asked. I want Mr. Purple and his associates. I suspect they don't even know your name, and nor do I, so you have nothing to worry about."

We both faced Len. I was holding my breath so hard, I could feel the blood running to my head.

"Raymond Portowski's an asshole," he said. "The mermaid wasn't in the car, but the moron asked me if I had any contacts he could sell it to. It's one thing to steal cars from unsuspecting idiots who leave them unlocked or run indoors with the engine still running, but it's totally another to rob old ladies. He deserves what he has coming."

Epilogue

February 13

"Let me come with you." Kat was making one last effort to plead her case to accompany Gordy to Immigration for her biometrics appointment. "I could wait outside." She was sitting at her kitchen counter Face-timing Gordy, both of them sipping steaming mugs of coffee.

"How will it look if I assure USCIS my marriage to Dana was bona fide and then as soon as I finish my fingerprints, I run out of the building and into the arms of another woman?"

"It *was* bona fide. They know that. They've seen the photographs and all the other proof. People fall out of love all the time. Why shouldn't immigrants? Anyway, who's going to be looking?"

"You never know. Dana had a friend who had an excellent job interview, and everyone on the panel raved about her and assured her she had the job. After she was done, she was so relieved she stood in the parking lot and lit up a joint. She had no idea that the HR department had spies in various places to see what candidates did before and after the interview. Of course, she didn't get the job. Maybe USCIS does the same thing."

Kat dunked a biscotti into her coffee. "I don't think the United States government has the same resources as a private corporation," said Kat, then laughed when she realized how absurd that sounded. Of course they did, though she very much doubted they'd use them for something like that. Still, she knew that where Gordy and immigration issues were concerned, it wasn't always a logical thing.

"Promise me, you'll text as soon as you're done."

"I promise."

"Oh and Gordy?" She grinned mischievously. "*Before* you get in the car, okay?"

"Too soon to joke about." Gordy's face glared at her from the screen.

"Sorry."

Gordy's face broke into a smile. "I'm just giving you a hard time. Since you were the one to get me out of that mess, you're allowed to make jokes about it." She glanced at her watch. "I have to go. I don't want Sammy to be late for school. Don't get worried if you don't hear anything for a while. They never take people in on time."

Kat had been so sure Gordy wouldn't agree to her going along, that she hadn't asked for any time off. Now she walked across town to work, her stomach in knots. Not because of Gordy's appointment but because of something else that was about to happen.

At The Garrett, she placed her phone on the counter-top where it was easily visible, and then thumbed through the latest *Gazette* while brewing another cup of coffee. She smiled when she saw a photograph of Officer Delgado handing over the silver mermaid to a beaming Mrs. Compton. He was flanked on either side by two officers who were looking at him with admiration. A separate article showed mugshots of Raymond Portowski and Wally Henderson under arrest and described the bust of a ring of car thieves, also thanks to Officer Delgado. No sign of Len Cardoza. Officer Del had kept his word about that. As she put the paper down, she noticed an advertisement with a smiling mechanic assuring customers that Wally's auto shop (now named Village Vehicles) was still in business, and she recognized the man as Pete. She'd have to be sure to bake him her best Black Forest cake. Without Pete, Gordy might still be in jail, or worse.

Kat forced herself to go through her usual routine, pulling out the ingredients she needed for the lunch menu and lining up the pots and pans. For once, she was alone. It was still early and Cindy wasn't in yet. She glanced up from time to time, looking out the window. When a lime-green Prius pulled in, her hands started to shake. A few minutes later, she left the kitchen and walked to the front office.

Frances was opening up her computer and looking at her to-do list.

"Do you have a minute?" Kat asked.

Frances glanced up, then jolted her head back.

"I'm not sure I do."

"I'll come back."

"It's okay. I have time. I just don't want to hear what you're about to tell me. It's written all over your face."

"Am I that transparent?"

"Right now you are." Frances paused. "When?"

"When what?" Kat was completely confused. She had a carefully rehearsed speech in her head, but Frances wasn't letting her give it.

"When are you leaving? Did someone give you a better offer? Because if so . . ."

"No. You know I love working for you. That's not why I'm leaving." Oh. She'd said it. Blurted it out. So much for the carefully crafted lead-up speech. She shifted her weight and tried to stand firmly instead of balancing on one leg. "I don't have another job, or even a date I want to leave. But I want you to know that I do have a plan. I want to have my own place, and I've started putting feelers out."

"Your own restaurant?"

"Not a restaurant exactly. A tea shop. I need to find the right space, and I'm happy to work for you until I do." Kat was scared Frances might tell her to get the hell out, that if she was leaving, she might as well do it right away. "I've been thinking about it for ages but I didn't think I had the courage to make the next move. These last couple of weeks, I've realized that I may be stronger than I know."

Frances glanced down at her desk, frowning. A moment later she got up and came around the other side of the table.

"I'm glad for you, Kat, truly I am. You can stay as long as you want."

They hugged and Kat felt the heavy weight she'd been carrying in her chest dissipate into the air. Until she started thinking about Gordy, and then everything tightened up again. The lunchtime crowd took every minute of her attention, and it was only when the last order had come in that she finally had a moment to glance at her phone. She read the text and let out such a loud whoop of happiness that Cindy came rushing in to find out what the fuss was about.

February 14

Kat and Gordy stood with Cindy, Jan and Deirdre in line with hundreds of impatient lesbians all clamoring to get into the Gulfport Casino (which wasn't a casino at all, but rather a giant social hall), for the women's social event of the year, the Lady in Red Ball. Kat fiddled nervously with the ruby cummerbund on the black tuxedo Cindy had persuaded her to rent.

"They may call me a redhead," she'd protested when Cindy first raised the idea, "but everyone knows my hair is ginger and that it clashes with real shades of red."

But neither Cindy nor Gordy would hear anything of it, and she was so high on happiness she didn't care if her hair clashed with every other item she was wearing. Although, truth be told, she'd been shocked by how much the tux suited her. After she assembled all the parts of it on the bed, she'd donned each one carefully, pulling the waistcoat down, adjusting the frills on the white shirt beneath it and making sure the bow tie was straight. She didn't own a full-length mirror, but she could see how she looked from the waist up when she ran some gel through her hair in the bathroom, and she was glad that she'd succumbed to wearing the tux. Gordy, of course, looked stunning. The blood-red camellia she'd tucked behind her luscious mahogany hair, perfectly matched the low-cut scarlet dress, which peeked through the unzipped leather jacket Gordy had worn the first day they met.

"How could I have lived so close to Gulfport for all these years and never known about the Lady in Red Ball?" Gordy gazed around, amazed at the array of women stomping their feet and slapping their arms to keep warm while they waited for the doors to open. Old and young, brown, black, and white, their outfits ran the gamut from long, formal gowns suitable for the Golden Globes, to shorts that could be worn for hiking, though most were elegantly dressed somewhere in between.

"Best-kept secret," said Jan. "We only tell the people we like."

Kat was glad all her friends approved of Gordy. It was as if she'd been one of them for a few years, not a few short weeks.

There was a sudden surge forward, and a loud voice asked those with tickets in hand to come to the right side of the doors and those with will-call to make their way left. Gordy started to move forward, but Kat put her hand on her arm. "Let's wait a bit longer. It's such a beautiful evening, there's no rush to go inside."

"We'll go ahead so we can grab a table," said Cindy, and Kat nodded. She stood with her arm around Gordy's waist drinking in the cool evening air and the faint scent of musk. She'd been looking forward to the dance but now that it was here, she was wiped out. It had been a long week, the longest in her life, although it was nothing compared to the week it had been for Gordy. She held Gordy's hand and looked out across Boca Ciega bay at the twinkling lights of distant buildings. Kat was about to turn and kiss her, when she felt a tap on her shoulder. She turned, and Gordy did too.

"You're here!" Gordy shouted excitedly. She bent down to kiss the woman in the wheelchair. Wynn was wearing rich red and purple loose-fitting pants and a matching shirt with billowing sleeves that covered the casts on her arms.

"Wouldn't miss it. I may not be able to dance the Florida Stroll but nothing was going to keep me away. Plus Tina was desperate to come." Wynn grinned at her daughter.

"Yeah, right. Hanging out with a bunch of old dykes dancing to 1980s music. My idea of a perfect Saturday night," said Tina, but her eyes were crinkled into a smile. She'd even switched out her shorts for black pants in honor of the occasion.

"How are all the body parts?" Kat asked, leaning down and hugging her friend.

"Everything's working well. Usually I use a walker. I can rest my cast on it to help me balance. But I was too nervous to try with so many people all around me. My doctor thinks I'm making remarkable progress for someone my age." She grimaced and used her head to put air quotes around the last part of the sentence. "Apparently he thought I'd be put out to pasture for the rest of my life. I wonder if he'll be ready to retire when he's only in his early sixties." She shuddered. "Let's go in. It's chilly out here."

Kat bent down and whispered in her ear. "Do you have it?"

"Oh! I almost forgot." Wynn looked up at Tina, who pulled something from the pocket of her jeans jacket and handed it to Kat. "Not only is my daughter a fantastic tennis player and a major help around the house, turns out she can also follow directions with pliers, wire, and gems."

Kat took the small square red velvet box decorated with Wynn's signature "W" design. "So you're not going out of business any time soon?"

"Between the insurance and the victim assistance money, I'll be able to manage until I'm back on my feet, or I guess I should say until my arms are back in action."

"And until that point, I'll be her permanent assistant," Tina said.

Wynn glared at her. "No decisions for now. Come on, wheel me inside," she said, and the two of them made their way toward the dance-hall entrance.

Kat turned toward Gordy. She took Gordy's hands and placed the velvet box so that they were cupped around it. Then she placed her own hands around Gordy's.

She was about to give her rehearsed speech, when Gordy stopped her.

"Hold on a minute," she said, pushing the little box back into Kat's hand.

Kat's heart sank. Was she moving too quickly?

Gordy shoved her hands deep into the pockets of her leather jacket then pulled something out of the left one. It was a velvet ring box identical to the one Kat had just given Gordy.

"I guess we really do have a lot in common," Gordy said as she added her box to the one Kat's hands were already cupping.

Kat smiled. Apparently, her timing was just right.

IF YOU ENJOYED THIS BOOK

Reviews are like giving a tip when you received good service. Positive online reviews make an enormous difference to writers. If you enjoyed this novel, please consider placing a review (a simple one-liner is fine!) on Amazon, Goodreads, Twitter, your Facebook page, and anywhere else where people might see it.

ABOUT THE AUTHOR

Alison R. Solomon grew up in England, and lived in Israel and Mexico before settling in the USA. Her debut novel, *Along Came the Rain*, was a Goldie finalist. Her short stories have been published in anthologies and magazines in the USA and Mexico. When she's not writing or providing social work consulting services, Alison can be found playing tennis or planning a trip. She lives with her wife and two rescue dogs in Gulfport, Florida.

Keep up on Alison's latest news and projects or join her newsletter at: www.AlisonRSolomon.com

Also Available from Alison R. Solomon

Did you wonder what had happened to Wynn Larimer and Kat Ayalon who both appeared to have histories not explained in this novel? Discover the answers in the two novels that serve as prequels to the Gulfport Mystery Series.

Along Came the Rain

Wynn Larimer would be the first to admit she has a bad memory and that lately it's been getting worse. But that doesn't explain how she has ended up in jail, accused of kidnapping two teenage foster kids. Now she's in the fight of her life to clear her name. Her burning question: who has framed her and why?

Sapphire Books, 2016.
ISBN (Print) 978-1-943353-27-9
ISBN (E-book) 978-1-943353-28-6

Devoted

Ashley Glynn knows there's more to her sister's untimely death than meets the eye. But as she investigates, Ashley is forced to confront the deep conflict within her own life between long-held religious beliefs and her sexuality. How can she discover the truth about her sister's death, if she can't face the truth about her own life?

Wild Girl Press, 2017
ISBN (Print) 978-0-9984400-0-2
ISBN (E-book) 978-0-9984400-1-9

Made in United States
North Haven, CT
25 July 2025